# Dead Spirits F

## by Geoffrey Sleight

Yesterday, upon the stair,
I met a man who wasn't there
He wasn't there again today
I wish, I wish he'd go away...

**Hughes Mearns**

# CHAPTER 1

THE PREVIOUS residents of the old farmhouse were lucky. They left just in time. The next couple to own the property were not so fortunate.

Its name, Fairview Farm, disguised a grim title that residents in the nearby village of Calbridge gave to the place. But that was one of the terrifying revelations yet to come in the unfolding story of the new owners.

Benjamin Telford, or Ben as he was known by friends and colleagues, had spent thirty years creating a successful housebuilding company. He was a hands-on man, starting as a building site labourer in his mid-twenties and eventually branching out to form his own construction business.

Now he was more office bound at High Wycombe, a busy town thirty five miles to the north west of London.

Even in his mid-fifties, Ben was still a strong, muscular man, betrayed only in age by greying hair and a furrowed brow. But his thoughts were turning towards taking an early retirement. He'd talked it over with his wife, Eleanor, on several occasions at their home situated not far from the company office.

They'd been married for twenty-five years. Ben had hired the attractive brunette with such beautifully innocent eyes shortly after he'd started his own company. Eleanor's young eyes might have looked innocent, but she was a shrewd accountant and a tempest of authority in her later role as business manager. She'd played a key role in the success of the business.

"There's an old farmhouse going cheap near a small village called Calbridge," said Ben as he sat on the sofa at home looking at properties for sale on his laptop. Eleanor sat beside him reading a book, the sound of the TV quiz show in front of them muted. She stopped reading to look across.

"It's in west Cornwall, not far from the sea," Ben continued, scrolling through the details. "Needs a bit of doing up, but I could make that my project. Might be ideal for our retirement plans."

"Wonder why it's going so cheap?" Eleanor's shrewd mind never lost its inquisitive grip, even though that young, innocent countenance had matured since with a few wrinkles. The rising tide of grey hair, however, was not to be tolerated, held back by the colouring of youthful brunette.

"Looks like someone's done work on the main farmhouse," Ben didn't appear to be taking in his wife's questioning, "but some outbuildings along the side need restoration. Might even be able to offer them as holiday lets. A bit of income." Ben had been office bound for too long. He yearned to use his practical building skills again. He turned to Eleanor.

"It's probably going cheap because of costly redevelopment work needed on the old storage outbuildings." He had been listening to his wife. "If I do it myself then the cost is a lot less."

Eleanor didn't feel entirely settled with the prospect, but it would be good if they could have an early retirement home not far from the sea in a beautiful countryside county where they'd spent holidays in the past, though this area and the village of Calbridge were unfamiliar to them. The couple decided Ben would take a few days off to visit the property and see the local estate agent.

That night Eleanor had an uneasy night's sleep. She dreamed her husband was calling for help from a doorway, his hand outstretched desperately trying to reach her, but being pulled back by some unseen force.

"What's the matter?"

She woke to see Ben sitting up beside her, wondering why she was crying out in distress.

"It's alright," she replied, rubbing her eyes, "just a bad dream."

Eleanor settled to sleep again, only to see her son, Michael, trying to comfort her in the loss of someone dear. Then her daughter Sophie joined him, dressed in sombre dark clothes, attempting to console her. Eleanor jolted waking from the dream, sitting upright on the bed. She stared into the darkness of the bedroom, the subdued glow of a street lamp shining through the curtains giving a little visibility.

"What's the matter ol' girl? What's troubling you?" For the second time Ben sat up beside her, this time placing his arm around her shoulders.

"It's okay. I'm just having some bad dreams," she rubbed her eyes again, as if that would wipe away the fear that had surfaced in her subconscious mind. "Didn't mean to disturb you."

"Probably that cheese and biscuits snack we had before going to bed," said Ben comforting her, "given you indigestion and bad dreams. Settle down my love. Everything's okay."

Her husband's warming words made Eleanor relax. She rested again, thoughts of her son Michael happily married to Australian girl, Lizzie, who he'd met when she'd come to the UK on a month long visit after graduating from university.

Michael was a whiz at accountancy, genetically inherited from his mother, and held the career qualification Lizzie planned to pursue. They clicked. He left his UK job to join her in Sydney, marrying a short time later and setting up their own business.

Eleanor missed him, but felt glad he was happy. Ben had harboured hopes that Michael would join the family business. But that's children for you he'd lamented, also glad his son was building a future.

Daughter Sophie was a single-minded woman, determined not to be drawn into distracting relationships. That is, until she met Leonard.

He was in complete contrast to the type of person everyone thought she would choose for a partner. A mild mannered man, inoffensive, non-argumentative and always happy to embrace another person's point of view. It obviously flummoxed Sophie. She had nothing to contest her fiery personality against. She fell madly in love with him, vowing always to protect him, and they'd been contentedly married for five years.

Sophie had moved from the local area too, now living a long distance away in Scotland, although not so distant as son Michael.

Eleanor drifted into sleep again, but somewhere in the back of her mind Ben's plans for the farmhouse retirement did not rest easily.

******

A COUPLE of days later Ben made the long journey to Calbridge to meet the local estate agent, Justin Turnbull. From the village he was driven to the farmhouse in the agent's car. The salesman was full of enthusiasm for the property.

"Heaps of potential," he described the place, pulling up on the farmstead's paved, red brick frontage.

Ben got out of the car and strode towards the dark oak front door. Justin caught up with him, adjusting his tie knot and smoothing his grey suit.

The original single-storey structure of the greystone farmhouse had been extended in local matching stone by the previous owner, adding first floor accommodation with a pitched slate roof.

Inside, the living room had been enlarged by demolishing the wall to an adjoining old pantry. It was a sizable area with a beamed ceiling. An inglenook fireplace added to the character of the setting.

The kitchen had been extended by taking out the wall of an old scullery. Modern units had been installed, but another part of its earlier look was maintained by a wide fire-

5

place, where a large cooking pot would have once hung over an open fire.

Another room, originally the bedroom, had been converted by the previous owner into a small lounge, retaining the old brick surround fireplace and red tiled floor. Ben instinctively felt there was something odd about the room, but he couldn't place it.

On the first floor the extension provided three bedrooms. Ideal thought Ben for friends and family to stay on visits.

There wasn't much improvement he could make inside the main property, which led him to question, like his wife, why it was on sale well below market value. The outbuildings at the side could be greatly improved, but that wouldn't account entirely for the low price.

"The last owners were wealthy people. Bought the property and did it up after it had been derelict for some years," Justin explained, "then I believe they decided to move abroad. Wanted a quick sale."

To Ben it sounded like an estate agent story, but he was captured by the setting. All around beautiful green meadows with crisp fresh air. Even though late autumn was approaching, the sun blazing in a clear blue sky radiated welcoming warmth through his being.

Beside the farmhouse a wide stony track led to several disused storage outbuildings lining the route, the old walls crumbling and the roofs on them virtually caved in.

The thought returned to Ben they'd be ideal to renovate and offer as holiday lets. Even in retirement he and Eleanor could earn some money from the summer season. The appeal of potential grew in his mind, pushing further away the curiosity of why the farmstead was being sold so cheaply.

Justin smiled inwardly, sensing his client was keen on the property, and glad that Ben's obvious attraction to the setting had distracted him from any close questioning that might lead to the farmhouse's dark history. The sales deal was sealed.

Back home, Eleanor still had misgivings about the purchase, but her husband had made many successful decisions and deals in the past, so she was guided by his plan. And it would be good to share more leisure time together after spending so many years on business, which on reflection had stolen a large chunk of their lives.

A couple of months later the sale completed. Ben gathered his sleeping bag and building equipment which he'd used a number of years back when he worked away from home on projects. The couple had agreed Eleanor would remain looking after the business in the office, while he set off in their Transit van to do some preliminary work preparing the outbuildings for renovation. The first step in the new venture.

But despite this growing positive in life, Eleanor could not rid the sense of dread that kept haunting her. The troubled dreams had continued. She waved goodbye to her husband on the driveway. A terrible omen of it being the last time she would see him alive made her shiver, as if she'd been clasped by a cold embrace from the grave.

------

BEN felt tired after the long, three-hundred mile drive to the west Cornwall farmhouse. He'd brought along a few home convenience comforts and set about heating a ready meal shepherd's pie in the microwave he'd installed in the kitchen.

He placed a couple of canvas chairs and a trestle table in the living room to make it look a little more homely, then settled himself at the table to eat the pie accompanied with a can of beer. He finished the meal and rested back in the chair starting to feel sleepy, his head slowly sinking towards his chest.

He woke with a jerk.

For a second Ben thought he'd heard a voice. Someone calling. He got up and opened the living room door into the hall, looking around.

"Hello," he called, wondering if a neighbour had come to the property to greet him. There was no reply. He must have imagined the sound while nodding off into sleep after dinner.

The early winter sun hovered low in the sky as twilight approached. Just time for Ben to carry out a bit of reconnaissance on the farmhouse outbuildings he'd earmarked for preliminary alteration. He could demolish the remaining sections of collapsing roofs, but work by his construction crews would be needed for later restoration.

As Ben walked down the track behind the farmhouse, checking the condition of the decaying buildings, the atmosphere seemed strangely quiet. He went inside one of them. The slate roof had almost entirely collapsed, rubble scattered across the floor, leaving the building open to the sky.

Flapping wings made him look up. Two brown hawks settled on top of the stone sidewall, staring at him inquisitively. Their sharp beaks, highly efficient at ripping apart small animals and carrion, seemed poised to launch at him. Ben suddenly felt vulnerable to attack. After a few moments the birds flapped their wings and took off, soon disappearing into the fading light of the sky.

He was a man with nerves of steel. But their presence had sent a shiver through him. He put it down to the chill air. Silly to feel unsettled by hawks. They don't usually bother humans. Returning to the farmhouse, he resolved to start demolishing the remaining section of the outbuilding's roof first thing in the morning.

Ben made a cup of coffee in the kitchen then realised it was time to ring Eleanor. She wanted to know he'd arrived safely. He dialled, but the call wouldn't connect. He saw the phone wasn't receiving a signal. This was an out of the way place and likely that connections were unreliable. Ben hoped his wife wouldn't worry. Especially if she was trying to call him. She knew he'd be okay he reasoned.

To while away a few evening hours he played some stored video games on the tablet he'd brought along. That, and a few beers kept him entertained in his loneliness. Then he made his way upstairs to the bedroom where he looked forward to settling with Eleanor when the place was furnished and they'd moved in.

For now a sleeping bag on the floor would have to do. The spartan bedding reminded him of his earlier days as a young man, staying in portakabins and mobile homes while working on contracts around the country.

Although he'd arranged for the farmhouse to be reconnected with electricity, he kept a torch handy beside him. From past experience he knew some of the more remote places could suffer power cuts if the weather turned stormy.

He turned off the light, a single bulb hanging from the centre of the ceiling on a short cord, and climbed into the sleeping bag. There were no curtains to shade the silver glow from the moonlight shining through the window overlooking the side track of the farmhouse.

Ben thought of Eleanor and all the days they could spend together enjoying a country life. After working so hard they deserved the chance of a more leisurely pace.

He must have fallen asleep, because the sound of voices made him open his eyes with a start. Surely there couldn't be anyone else in the place? He sat up listening intently. The silence almost hummed. The moonglow seemed to cast a strange atmosphere of another world not quite within earthly grasp.

After a few moments he dismissed the sense of something not being right, deciding he'd just heard voices in a dream, and settled down. Soon after, he awoke to the voices again. They were coming from downstairs. Maybe it was another dream, but he decided to check.

Ben got up and flicked on the light switch. It didn't work. The room remained in moonlight. A power failure already? He grabbed the torch just as the sound of voices now came from the side track below the window. He crossed to it and looked down to see the shadowy outbuildings in the moonglow, but no presence.

His heart began pumping quickly. He switched on the torch to search downstairs. Perhaps a property left unoccupied attracted tramps for a comfortable night's accommodation.

He opened the bedroom door and shone the torch beam along the landing, making his way to the stairs. At the top he directed it down the stairwell. It lit a well rounded, middle-aged woman standing at the bottom. She wore a dark grey dress with a white apron and linen mob cap. The clothing appeared to be from an age long past. She stared at him with a calculating smile, assessing him like a victim for a terrible fate. Ben almost dropped the torch in shock.

As he stared back, her image disappeared and the torchlight displayed just the empty flagstone hall floor where she'd stood. He remained still, his mind confused, attempting to take in what he'd seen. He didn't believe in ghosts...and yet?

Shining the torch around into the dark below, there was no sign of any other intruder. Cautiously he made his way down the stairs to check the rooms and ensure the front door and all the windows were locked.

Without electric lighting the darkness outside of the torch beam seemed to hide unseen eyes watching his every move. Ben had never felt a sense of fear and dread like this before. He kept insisting to himself there must be a logical explanation for the figure of the woman he'd just witnessed.

After checking the living room and kitchen, he entered the lounge at the end of the hallway. A window overlooking the front of the property allowed just enough moonglow to faintly light the room. Standing at the open door, an invisible presence seemed to loom inside the room, gloating at him, a cold foreboding of something unnatural. Ben shivered as he looked around, then hurriedly closed the door to shut it out.

Doing his best to dismiss these illogical fears, he satisfied himself the place was locked and no-one else was in the farmhouse. Then he made his way back upstairs to the bedroom, beginning to wonder if he'd made the right decision in buying the property. Had it been going cheap for reasons the estate agent omitted to explain? That it was haunted? Nonsense. There were no such things as ghosts, he reasoned. No-one had ever properly proved they existed, he insisted to himself.

Entering the bedroom he saw the ceiling light was back on. He persuaded himself the cause of the blackout was a power failure. And maybe he'd still been half asleep and just imagined the woman at the bottom of the stairs. That would be a much more logical explanation he convinced himself as he settled back down in the sleeping bag.

# CHAPTER 2

THE farmhouse appeared a completely different place in the morning. Bright sunlight streaming through the windows drove away all the ghoulish fears of the night.

Ben checked his phone to see if it might now be receiving a signal so he could call his wife, but there was still no connection. She would probably realise there was a problem with phone signals in an out of the way place like this he thought. She wouldn't worry.

He had enough provisions to keep going for a few days, and after making scrambled egg for breakfast, washed down with a warming cup of tea, he set about the day's work.

By late afternoon Ben had demolished the remaining roof of an outbuilding and cleared the rubble into a pile outside, ready for when the time came to call in a local waste disposal company. Before going back to the farmhouse he walked to the end of the track, where a wooden gate bounded on each side by a wire fence opened on to the green acreage that came with the property.

Meadows stretched before him. Settings where he imagined farmers who'd owned the property in years past had once grazed cattle or sheep, or cultivated it for crops. The land had been left fallow for some time, nature taking its course with once neat hedgerows now over grown into bushy clusters. One day he'd have to get that sorted out, but for now the building project took priority.

Ben made his way back to the farmhouse and after showering in the bedroom's en-suite went down to the kitchen to make a coffee. As he leaned back against the counter taking a drink from the cup, a weird sensation of not being alone in the farmhouse came over him. He placed the cup on the kitchen table and walked into the living room.

Apart from the trestle table and canvas chairs, all was empty. But the sense of a presence remained. Entering the nearby lounge, the room stood empty. Ben began to reassure himself that the events of the previous night had spooked his mind, left him prone to imaginings.

The sun was now dipping to the horizon and rays of a gold sunset lit the forecourt through the lattice window. Satisfied there was no-one in the room, he was about to leave when a woman suddenly materialised from the wall at the side. He froze. She walked across as if heading somewhere, then seeing him stopped. Her brown hair was tied back in a bun. She wore a long, dark green dress that brushed the floor. She gazed at Ben from her chubby face, fixing him with inquisitive eyes.

"I'd get out of here if I were you," she said to him. "They'll be returning soon and they won't let you escape." The woman continued walking and dissolved through the opposite wall.

Ben's heart pumped fit to burst. For several minutes he stood in shock. Now he was convinced he'd seen a ghost. Another woman whose clothes seemed to belong to a past era. What the hell was going on here? What had gone on here?

The coffee was not enough to settle his nerves. He returned to the kitchen and took a beer from the cupboard. A long, hard drink of the liquid helped relax him a little. He checked his phone to see if there was now a signal. None showed. He wanted to speak to Eleanor and hear her reassuring voice. The realisation that spectres haunted the farmhouse deepened his sense of isolation.

His instinct was to climb into the Transit van and get away from the place as fast as possible. Something very strange must have taken place here.

Ben made his way upstairs to the bedroom and began packing his things. In the process his mood changed.

"No!" he shouted aloud. "I will not be driven away from the place I bought and own. Ghosts? Spirits? I must be losing my mind. There are no ghosts."

As his fury subsided, doubts started to creep in again. And although his defiance remained, he couldn't forget the warning that had come from the woman in the lounge, even though he tried to convince himself she'd been a figment of his imagination. 'They won't let you escape'.

In the evening he passed the time once more playing games on the tablet in the living room and drinking a few more beers. Tomorrow he would carry on with the work preparing the outbuildings for renovation. Ben was determined his fears would not get the better of him.

That night he checked the locks on the downstairs windows and front door were secure, then made his way upstairs.

The sky featured no moon on his second night, covered by high cloud. The bedroom disappeared into total darkness as he turned out the light and switched off the torch guiding him to the sleeping bag. Ben felt uneasy and wanted to turn the light on again, but the thought of being frightened in the dark made him feel ridiculous as if he was degenerating into childhood. He resolved to leave the light off and in a short while drifted into sleep.

A noise made him open his eyes. It sounded like the flapping of bird wings. He stared into the darkness. Then he heard someone laughing. A man's laugh, as if gloating over a victim. Ben sprang upright in the sleeping bag.

A few feet away a man with long straggly hair stood staring at him. He wore a white shirt soiled grey by dusty dirt, black shapeless trousers spattered with mud. His eyes shone piercingly from a deeply lined, unshaven face.

"I suppose you're looking for work here," the illuminated spectre spoke in a condescending tone. Ben sat transfixed. "Start at first light, and if you're lucky my wife will give you a meal." The spectre stared at Ben for a moment longer then evaporated. The pitch darkness returned.

Ben continued sitting, his mind desperately trying to dismiss the vision as an illusion. This time he was unable to avoid the truth.

"This place *is* bloody haunted," he said aloud.

Climbing out of the sleeping bag he switched on the light, thankful that it was working, then went downstairs to the kitchen. Taking a beer from the cupboard, he downed it rapidly in an attempt to calm his shaking nerves.

He decided not to go back to the bedroom and attempt to sleep in there again. He glanced at the clock he'd placed on the counter. It was nearly four-thirty in the morning. He went outside and breathed the cool air. It was refreshing. Glancing at the Transit van, it was all he could do to resist climbing in and driving back home. But he wasn't going to give up so easily. Surely something could be done to rid the farmhouse of these unwelcome visitors?

He went back inside to the living room and sat in one of the canvas chairs, resting. He dozed lightly. Deeper rest evaded him. As the dawn light began to creep in, he came to a decision. He would go into the nearby village and ask the estate agent who'd sold him the property for more information about the place. The farmhouse's earlier history.

Ben was beginning to feel a fool that he hadn't made more local enquiries about the property before he'd bought it. He'd been captured by the beautiful countryside surroundings and thoughts of spending happy days there with Eleanor.

******

THE estate agent's office was situated in the high street with a grocery shop, post office and newsagent nearby. On the opposite side of the narrow road stood The Wheatsheaf pub. The remainder of the high street was lined with granite stone cottages and a side road sloped upwards to the old church of St Peter's, its clock tower rising majestically above the setting.

Ben entered the office, asking the young woman receptionist for Justin Turnbull, the man who'd sold him the property.

"Mr Turnbull is out on a property viewing with a client," she informed him. "He'll be back shortly. Can I ask what it's about?"

"No, don't worry. I'll call in later," he replied.

Ben walked along the high street, now able to pick up a phone signal in the village. He rang Eleanor.

"Thank God you've called," she greeted him. "I was worried sick something had happened. Another hour and I was going to call the police."

Ben assured Eleanor he was well and explained why it hadn't been possible to contact her until now. But he was in a quandry. Should he tell his wife of the strange manifestations at the farmhouse? He didn't want to worry her. Not admit he'd probably made a blunder buying the property. No, he would sort it out. She didn't have to know at this moment.

"I'm making good progress," said Ben. "I think we'll both be very happy here." He only wished he felt as confident as the reassurance pouring from him. "I"ll be coming into the village fairly often, so I'll let you know how it's going."

They chatted for a little longer and ended the conversation with Ben solemnly promising to keep in regular contact.

Back at the estate agent, Justin Turnbull had returned and came out of his office greeting Ben with a well rehearsed oily smile and firm handshake. Inviting him inside, he beckoned his visitor to a chair while settling himself behind the desk.

Ben explained the visitations he'd experienced at the farmhouse and demanded to know if the property was reputed to be haunted. Is that why it was sold to him so cheaply?

Turnbull gazed at his former client as if he was mad.

"The place has no history of hauntings so far as I'm aware," he played down the possibility.

Ben was not convinced he was being told the truth. The agent's eyes seemed to be masking an inner knowledge. He realised Turnbull would not be forthright even if he was aware of some dubious history attached to the farmhouse. He couldn't know that Justin Turnbull was well aware of the property's local reputation for horrific hauntings. The agent had sold the property and he couldn't care less beyond that point.

Ben left feeling totally dissatisfied with the meeting. Turnbull was hiding something, but without physically forcing it out of him he knew he'd learn nothing more down that avenue of pursuit.

Fate unexpectedly delivered more information when he entered the grocery store in the high street to buy some provisions.

"You live at the farmhouse, don't you?" asked the smiling, middle-aged woman behind the counter. Ben looked at her in surprise, which confirmed the answer.

"It's alright," she said, "news of new people in the area travels fast round here." The woman totted up the cost of his purchases and Ben placed them in a bag.

"Getting on okay there?" she enquired further, in a way that seemed to be searching for a negative reply. Ben nodded, which didn't appear to satisfy her.

"Nothing sort of...?" she left the sentence hanging.

Ben realised the woman knew something about the farmhouse and this could open a new line of information.

"Nothing sort of what?" he questioned.

"Oh, nothing." The woman decided she wasn't going to elicit anything of gossipy interest from him. Ben paid for his purchases, now knowing she was bursting for some feedback.

"If you want to know, I've seen some ghosts there," he said casually. The woman's jaw dropped.

"It's true then," she uttered, unable to stem her reaction. Then she shook her head. "You're having me on."

Ben stared back.

"No, I really have seen ghosts there."

For a few moments silence hovered. Then a torrent opened.

"Everyone round here knows the farmhouse is meant to be haunted, though no-one locally has seen them. But those who've lived there," she paused, "they don't hang about for long." The woman suddenly felt she'd said too much. "Sorry, I didn't mean to worry you."

"It's okay, I'm not worried," Ben replied, hiding the fact that now he was truly concerned. "I just want to know a bit more about the place."

"Well, Marian Armstrong's your woman for local history in this area," the shopkeeper told him. "She lives at nine Sheepfield Dell. It's a cottage just off the high street about a hundred yards down," she pointed left. Ben thanked her and left the shop, deciding to pay the woman a visit before returning to the farmhouse.

The narrow cobblestone road off the high street was lined on each side with more granite stone cottages, net curtains covering the ground floor windows along its length. He reached number nine and rapped the door knocker. There was no reply. He tried again, but still no answer. He'd have to call again another time.

About to walk away, Ben caught sight of a slightly stooped elderly woman with long, grey hair approaching. She wore a threadbare black overcoat and carried a shopping bag.

"You looking for me?" the woman called to Ben.

"Marian Armstrong?" he called back.

"The very same," she replied in a well spoken accent. "What can I do for you?" She reached the door, putting down the shopping bag and reaching for keys in her overcoat pocket.

Ben explained he was interested in the history of the farmhouse.

"Oh, a very interesting place," she stared at him through baggy, wrinkled eyes, a large wart on her cheek catching his attention for a moment.

"Come on in," she opened the door. "I'll put the kettle on."

Ben followed into a gloomy, narrow hallway, the wallpaper faded and the varnish on the stairway bannister almost bare to the woodwork, the dark red carpet on the stairs and hall floor worn down to the stitching.

"You'll have to excuse the place," she said. "My husband refuses to maintain it." She omitted to say her husband had died ten years earlier, refusing to accept in her mind that he was no longer around.

"Go into the sitting room while I make us some tea," she indicated a door at the end of the hallway. Ben walked down and entered.

In this room the once light yellow walls were now browned with bare patches of plaster scattered across the surface. A floral patterned sofa looked faded and sagging. The image of a confident, grey-suited young man smiled from a photo frame placed in the centre of the mantelpiece. Ben assumed he was her husband captured on film in earlier years.

Marian entered the room wearing a tired black cotton dress. She carried a tray with a pot of tea, cups and saucers and a plate of biscuits, placing it on a side table beside the sofa.

"That's my husband Ernest," Marian noticed Ben looking at the photos. "We've aged a bit since then," she laughed. Pouring the tea, she beckoned Ben to the sofa.

"Come and sit beside me and tell me what you want to know."

Ben accepted the invitation and sat down, doing his best to ignore the spring in the dilapidated furniture pressing into his backside.

He told Marian he'd just moved into the farmhouse and had experienced some strange events, fully expecting the woman to scoff at them as imaginings. But she listened intently and seemed to take his words seriously.

When he finished she said nothing for a moment, pondering. Then took a sip of tea before replying.

"Yes the place does have a bit of history," she said.

"Maybe I should have checked it out on the internet before buying," Ben reprimanded himself.

"Good heavens you won't find anything about its past on that internet thing," Marian raged. "Books, that's where real knowledge can be found. An abomination of Satan is that internet," she was not impressed by modern times.

"There's a book I have that contains information about Fairview Farm," the woman calmed herself, sticking to the subject in hand.

"Of course, that's a modern name that was given to the place. I think the locals in earlier times called it Dead Spirits Farm. But hold on, I've got the book in the other room. I'll get it." She rose from the sofa and left.

Ben began to wonder why the farmhouse had once been named Dead Spirits Farm. It was not exactly encouraging.

A few minutes later Marian returned carrying a book and wearing pink framed spectacles. She settled on the sofa beside him opening a page and pointing to some text.

"Yes, this is the piece recorded by a local historian some years ago. It refers to the owner of the farm back in the 1850s employing passing travellers to work on the farm. Vagrant labourers with no homes of their own earning a subsistence living." Marian moved her finger down the page.

"Yes, by this account the owners, John Trevallion and his wife Anne, treated the workers cruelly, paying them only with meagre meals and rough sleeping accommodation in the rat infested outbuildings." Marian turned the page looking further down the text.

"Ah yes, now towards the end of the 1850s rumours were growing that passing vagrants working there over a number of years simply disappeared. Some put it down to the nature of vagrants. Others suspected something evil was happening."

Ben found himself feeling less comfortable with the idea of living at the farm, but was determined not to be put off by what might just be country legends, despite his own strange experiences at the property. He'd invested money in it and was determined to make his plan work.

Marian flipped through a few more pages.

"Now in 1859," she continued, "a young woman living in the village, who helped the farm owners out with cleaning jobs, suddenly disappeared. There were extensive searches, but she was never found. Rumours went round the village that John Trevallion and his wife had murdered her. After a few weeks, a lynch mob attacked the farm and hanged the couple from a nearby tree." Marian closed the book.

The part about the young woman in the narrative being murdered, raised the image in Ben's mind of the female spectre he'd seen in the lounge.

Marian took another sip of tea and went on to tell of later events she retained in memory about the history of the farm.

"From 1860, new farmers occupied the property, but always abandoned it. This went on periodically for more than a hundred years. Then about two years ago the farm was bought by a wealthy man. It had fallen into a state of disrepair and he had it restored and modernised. However, not long after he and his wife abandoned it, and the farmhouse was left unoccupied until you bought it."

Ben realised from the dates that he was the next person to buy the property, Now serious doubts were surfacing in his mind. The farm obviously had a dark history attached.

"I think the tree John Trevallion and his wife Anne were hanged from is still there," Marian continued. That was another piece of information Ben wished he'd never heard.

"And, of course," she added, "rumours of the place being haunted have grown."

She offered him a biscuit from the tray, but he declined. His appetite was diminishing from what he'd heard.

"There's no hard evidence of these events taking place," Marian reassured him. "Country folk, especially back in those days, could come up with some very colourful, inaccurate tall stories."

Ben wasn't sure if she'd said that because she believed it, or was just trying to allay any fears it might cause him. He changed the subject.

"Excuse me, if you won't mind me saying so, but you're accent doesn't sound as though you come from these parts," Ben was curious.

"You're right, I don't come from here," Marian sat back on the sofa. "I was a senior lecturer teaching English and medieval history at Oxford University, a good distance from here. My husband was a Fellow there."

Ben was impressed, it was one of Britain's top universities.

"We decided on a simpler life when our children grew up. We always loved this part of the world, so we upped sticks and moved here to live. Smaller income, working on research and educational publications, but happiness from the stress," she explained.

Ben finished his tea and thanked Marian for her time.

"Anything else you want to know, don't hesitate to call on me," she smiled as Ben left.

Walking back to the car, he met the woman from the grocery store sweeping the pavement outside her shop.

"Did you see Mrs Armstrong?" she asked.

"Yes, very helpful."

"She's a funny ol' thing, but very kind," the shopkeeper ventured her opinion. "Sad though."

Ben had been about to walk on. Her last comment made him stop. The woman could see she'd grabbed his interest and now rested, clasping the top of the broom handle as she related the tale.

"Marian was on holiday with her husband in Italy. About ten years ago now. They were on a coach that crashed. She survived, but her husband was killed." The woman clutched the broom ready to start sweeping again. "Marian thinks he's still alive. The shock drove her a bit mad. Normal in everything else though." She gave a sad smile.

Ben was numbed by the story. He'd obviously had no idea. He walked on as the shopkeeper took to sweeping again. Now it figured why her home was in such a mess. Marian really thought that her husband was failing to maintain it. That everything was going on as usual. He pledged to himself that when he'd made some progress on the farmhouse outbuildings, he would offer to redecorate her cottage as a gesture of goodwill.

# CHAPTER 3

ON return to the farmhouse, Ben heated a ready meal shepherd's pie in the microwave and after eating set about working on the restoration again.

He was perched at the top of a ladder resting against the sidewall of an outbuilding, when he saw two men a short distance away along the track. One held a shovel and the other a pitchfork. Their shirt sleeves were rolled up and their trousers spattered with mud.

"Can I help you?" Ben called to them, presuming they were workers from a nearby farm. The men stared at him, but made no reply.

He climbed down the ladder to approach them. They continued staring at him.

"Get back to work you lazy bastards!" a thunderous voice from behind made Ben jump. He swung round. There was no-one in sight. As he turned back to the men they'd disappeared. The track stood empty. Ben wandered up and down it, peering into the other outbuildings searching to see if anyone was present. He was alone. He started to wonder if he'd imagined the event.

Then the grim thought came to him. He'd seen spectres. The visitations were not confined to hours of the night. Again his instincts pressed him to leave, but he was determined not to be driven away. The living should prevail. The dead should remain as that. Somehow he would overcome this problem. But the thought of spending another night in the property began to fill him with dread.

When night did come, he settled into his sleeping bag with the trusty torch by his side and the room light left on. Laying there it came into his mind to consult one of those ghost hunter types of people. He'd seen programmes about ghost hunting on TV, but had always put it down to phoney baloney, as he'd described it to his wife, Eleanor.

Now his mind was less cynical about unearthly manifestations. Raw experience had put him on the road to conversion. Perhaps a ghost hunter could work out the source of the visitations. The reason. Advise how to isolate it. There was no doubt it was attached to this farmer, John Trevallion and his wife, who it seemed had done something horrific here. The dead would be put away in their place. In the grave where they belonged.

\*\*\*\*\*\*

Ben shot up in his sleeping bag woken by terrifying howls and yells coming from downstairs. Cries of horror.

"No, don't kill me I beg you!" A man's pitiful voice rang out, followed by a woman's scream for mercy rising above the horrific commotion.

He stared into the darkness. The room light was out. His hand frantically searched for the torch beside him. Grabbing it, he turned on the beam. The harrowing cries ceased. Silence fell like an all embracing shroud. Ben decided to investigate.

The landing light wouldn't come on. It appeared there had been another power cut. He braced himself against seeing another figure standing in the beam of torchlight at the bottom of the stairway like the other night. But there was none. He descended.

The darkness outside the beam of light again seemed to contain unseen spectres. His blood chilled and his nerves tensed. He swept the light across the living room and kitchen, fearful every second of picking out a spirit standing there. The thought of seeing a living intruder would be less daunting than highlighting a ghost. The rooms were empty.

He approached the lounge growing even more tense. This room gave him a terrible sense of foreboding. The setting where he'd seen the young woman appearing and issuing the warning to leave. Tonight, no moonlight shone into the room.

With a sweep of the torch, for a second he thought he saw a shadowy figure standing beside the brick surround fireplace, flames flickering in the grate. But the image was gone. The atmosphere hung threateningly. Quickly he shut the door to mask the sensation.

The commotion he'd heard certainly hadn't come from any living person in the property. That left only one conclusion. Again Ben considered the option of abandoning the farmhouse, but he was not a man to be easily turned away. He'd never succumbed to running away before and was damned if he'd do it now. He never considered the possibility that he was heading towards becoming damned.

Making his way back upstairs, the landing light suddenly came on. The light in the bedroom was also restored. It dawned on him that the power cuts seemed to coincide with nightly visitations, and were perhaps beyond just coincidence.

Ben settled again in his sleeping bag, but sleep evaded him. Every time he began to relax, creaking joists in the property or a distant owl hooting made him start in fear of another spectral visitor.

He set off early next morning to the village where he could connect to a phone signal. He hadn't noticed on his first visit that there was a small cafe further down the high street. He could ring his wife and search for a ghost hunter on his phone while enjoying a coffee.

A bell clanged as he opened the door. The glass fronted counter contained a selection of cakes, but there was no-one behind it. The cafe accommodated several tables, though as yet no other customers. Ben waited for a few moments wondering if anyone had heard the bell, then a young woman appeared from a door behind the counter looking flustered, hands behind her back tying on an apron.

"Good morning," she greeted him with a hurried smile. It seemed to Ben the cafe didn't expect any customers this early in the day. He glanced at his watch. It was just after seven thirty.

"Passing through?" the woman enquired as he ordered his coffee. Her light brown hair and the inquisitive gleam in her eyes reminded him a little of his daughter Sophie.

"No, I'm the new owner of Fairview Farm," Ben announced. The gleam in her eyes faded, replaced by inner thoughts of the farm's dark legend.

"Settling in okay?" this question was loaded, now seriously inquisitive.

"It's an interesting place," Ben replied enigmatically. He could see she was hoping to hear strange tales about the property, but at that moment he didn't feel inclined to give her the satisfaction.

"I'll bring your coffee over to you. Make yourself comfortable," the woman turned to make the beverage.

Ben sat at a table near the window and began an internet search for ghost hunters on his phone. He was surprised how many of them advertised their services. It was pot luck choosing one. No way to tell who was the best. He selected the ghost hunter nearest to his location in a town about twenty miles away. But first he called Eleanor.

"Just having some breakfast," she sounded sleepy. He assured her all was going well, continuing to hide the supernatural events at the farmhouse.

"Is all going well back at the office?" he enquired.

"Yes, running more smoothly than ever without you around," she laughed. Hearing her laughter raised Ben's spirits considerably. It was one of the typical jokey stabs she made at him from time to time. But her next remark put him on guard.

"I've been thinking, why don't I come and join you for a few days. Ken Wainwright the office manager could take the helm for a while?" Eleanor suggested.

Ben didn't answer immediately. He'd love his wife's company, but didn't want to expose her to the terrors he'd known at the farmhouse. He needed time to sort that out.

"It's a bit rough and ready here. You wouldn't be comfortable," Ben attempted to discourage her.

"We used to rough it in our earlier days. It'd bring back memories," Eleanor insisted.

"I don't think you should come here yet," Ben replied tersely. He hadn't intended that tone.

Eleanor was silent for a while before replying.

"Okay. If you don't want me there."

"I didn't mean it like that."

"No, it's okay. I understand."

"I love your company, but I want to make a bit more progress before you come," Ben attempted to placate her.

"I'd better get on now," Eleanor sounded distinctly frosty.

"I'm not trying to turn you away..." he didn't finish. His wife had hung up.

"Everything alright?" the cafe owner approached Ben with the coffee. He reddened with embarrassment. She must have worked out that he'd had a disagreement with probably his wife or partner at the other end of the call.

"Yes, everything's fine," he said, knowing it sounded entirely unconvincing.

"You planning to live at the farmhouse?" the woman probed further, placing the coffee on the table.

That's the plan," he replied, then decided to go on the offensive. "Why? Is there something wrong with the place?" The woman was unprepared for return probing.

"No, not really," she stuttered. "There's always been rumours about the place."

"What rumours?" Ben drove home with the questioning.

"Well..."

The doorbell clanged as an elderly woman wearing a green headscarf entered.

"Must go." The cafe owner looked relieved by the chance to serve her new customer.

Ben suddenly felt guilty by rounding on the young woman. The fallout with his wife had upset him. He didn't mean to take out his tension on an innocent. She was just curious about his experience of a place that was obviously reputed to be haunted.

When he finished his drink he made a point of thanking the owner to show he was not an unfriendly person. She was standing beside a table chatting to the other customer.

"Great cup of coffee," he smiled.

She returned an uncertain smile, not quite sure about this newcomer to the village. The other woman stared at him from beneath her headscarf as if witnessing an alien curiosity. The moment he left the cafe and closed the door, he could sense their tongues wagging about him.

He walked a short distance down the high street and made the call to the ghost hunter. It was not a subject he wanted to discuss in range of prying ears at the cafe.

"Have you seen the presence, or do you just think there's a strange feeling about the place?" enquired the ghost hunter. "Have items been thrown around? Poltergeists?"

Ben explained his experiences at the farmhouse.

"Definitely sounds haunted," came the reply.

"Can you help me to track down the cause?" Ben wanted to know.

"I'm certain I can help you with that."

"When can you do it?"

"As it happens, I'm between appointments. I can come later today."

Ben felt relieved on hearing that. He'd been toying with the idea of staying in a local bed and breakfast rather than spend another night with the visitations. If he could sort out the problem quickly, that would be good.

"I'll need to stay the night," the ghost hunter explained, Ben pointed out there was no proper accommodation yet at the farmhouse.

"I'll be working not sleeping. Don't worry about a bed."

Ben agreed the price and gave him the address. The man would arrive at eight that evening. The thought of having some company in the place was heartening.

\*\*\*\*\*\*

THE ghost hunter arrived carrying a large case of equipment.

"Andrew Tripp," he introduced himself, shaking Ben's hand. His shiny bald head carried vestiges of black hair on each side that once covered the entire surface. The man smiled, peering at his client through the thick lenses of brown rimmed spectacles. He was immaculately dressed in a dark suit.

Ben made coffee, then took him on a tour of the farm-house. The ghost hunter held an electronic magnetic field detector

"This can help to narrow down areas of paranormal activity," he explained, noticing the puzzled expression on Ben's face. Andrew murmured to himself while assessing information from the detector as they worked their way through the property.

"Ahh," his eyes lit up studying the device when they arrived in the lounge. "Definite signs in here."

Ben was impressed. This was the room that held the most potent sensation of something unnatural. The room where he'd seen the spirit girl issuing her warning to him. The main bedroom, where the man had appeared in the night, was another location of the detector reacting, though not strongly like the lounge.

"I shall monitor several locations through the night, but will set up the night vision camcorder in the lounge for a start," Andrew explained, taking a camera and tripod from his case as well as a thermometer to measure changes in room temperature that could signal a presence.

Ben offered the man the hospitality of a canvas chair in the living room and they sat chatting for a while. He drank a beer while Andrew remained strictly on coffee to keep a clear head.

"Don't you get frightened by spirits?" Ben was curious.

"Some of them can be a bit unnerving, but of course they're dead. Can't do the living any harm," he replied, completely assured. "And most aren't really ghosts at all.

Just the workings of people with overactive imaginations, seeing or hearing things that aren't really there."

Ben wasn't sure if the ghost hunter might be classifying him in that category, but said nothing.

"Right, I'd better set to work," said Andrew looking at his wrist watch showing just after ten.

"Do you want me to help you?" Ben offered.

"No, it's okay. You get some rest. I'll call if I need any help, but it should be fine." Andrew made his way to the lounge, while Ben finished his beer before going upstairs. Tonight he would sleep in the second bedroom, as the ghost hunter wanted to visit the main bedroom later where the man offering Ben work had materialised.

As he settled in his sleeping bag he felt relaxed for the first time since arriving, knowing he was in the company of someone who seemed entirely immune to the fear of paranormal activity. Soon he fell asleep.

He woke to the sound of movement downstairs. A hurried clattering of objects. He lay there for a moment supposing that Andrew was moving equipment around. The place fell silent. A minute later he heard a car engine starting on the forecourt. A vehicle driving away. He got up and quickly putting on his T-shirt and trousers descended the stairs.

"Andrew?" he called. There was no reply. Ben opened the front door. The man's car was gone.

Fear gripped him. What had happened? Why had the ghost hunter rapidly left without a word? It appeared he'd been deserted.

He searched the rooms, approaching the lounge with caution. The door was half open, but no light inside. Part of him wanted to look, but the greater part warned him against it. Gingerly he reached out with his arm to close the door, but couldn't resist looking. He flicked on the switch, dreading what he might see. The room was empty, but the atmosphere filled with unseen threat. The farmhouse lights suddenly flickered. Ben's heart was leaping. Darkness right now could cause it to give out. Thankfully the light remained on. Swiftly he pulled the door shut.

Staying in the place was becoming impossible. More and more his inclination was to just leave the accursed property. Write it off as a bad investment and head home for the future. But more and more he grew angry at the thought of being driven out of something that was rightfully his own. He couldn't lose sight of overcoming the problem. The dead had no place to interfere with the living. He would fix it.

In the meantime though, to be on the safe side, he resolved to find new accommodation in the village. He'd seen signs at some cottages offering bed and breakfast. He could rest there in the evening and work on the outbuildings during the day. At least he could enjoy comfortable nights that way while giving him time to seek a solution.

Ben decided to spend the rest of the night in the Transit van. He could lay out the sleeping bag in the back. Hardly the height of luxury, but preferable to suffering another haunting. Before transferring to the van he rang the ghost hunter to try and find out why he'd left so rapidly, but only got a recorded message. He'd try again later in the morning.

*\*\*\*\*\*\**

BEN could only get small snatches of sleep in the back of the vehicle. He returned to the farmhouse a few hours later when it was light in order to wash and get something to eat. Then he set off for the village.

He chose a cottage in the high street with a bed breakfast sign a short distance from the newsagent and rang the doorbell. A grey-haired woman in a navy blue dress answered, peering at him inquisitively. It wasn't an unfriendly gaze, but not a full welcome.

"Yes?" she quizzed.

Ben explained he was looking for accommodation.

"I only do it in the summer," she replied, "holiday time."

"I saw your sign in the window."

"Forgot to take it down," she eyed him up and down, making an assessment of the stranger on her doorstep. Ben was about to leave.

"I'll put you up for a day or two," she said, deciding some out of holiday season income could come in handy.

"Thank you. I'll get my things from the van," Ben smiled his gratitude.

He settled into a small room on the first floor of the cottage, plain and simple in layout with a wardrobe, dressing table, armchair and single bed, but it was like a palace compared to the unfurnished conditions at the farmhouse. And more importantly, a refuge from the supernatural.

While there he rang Eleanor who fortunately no longer sounded frosty towards him. He made the excuse he was staying in a bed breakfast so that life was a bit more comfortable for him without mentioning the real reason for his relocation. After talking to her, he was about to call the ghost hunter when the man himself rang.

"I'm so sorry I deserted you," Andrew began. "If I were you, I'd leave the farmhouse as quickly as possible," he warned.

This didn't sound good to Ben.

"Why, what happened?"

Andrew took a moment to reply, his voice loaded with fear.

"I have never experienced such a sense of evil in a place," he said. "At around two in the morning in the lounge, my meter readings went haywire, the room temperature plummeted. Then a young woman dressed in clothes like more than a hundred years or so ago appeared from the side wall. She warned me to leave quickly." Andrew paused. Ben could hear him catching his breath as he relived the memory.

"Then she disappeared and a man with the most terrifying, manic eyes I've ever seen came out of the wall and stared viciously at me. He began to approach. He had a long bladed knife in his hand...." the ghost hunter paused, remaining silent.

"Hello?" Ben thought he'd hung up.

"It's alright, I'm here," Andrew replied. "I was convinced he was going to kill me. I felt he was taking over my mind. Preventing me from moving. Then the apparition disappeared. I fear I would have been killed if the spirit hadn't suddenly gone."

"Did you catch it all on your camcorder?" asked Ben.

"That's the strange thing. I did. But back here at home I replayed it and the recording is completely blank. No sound, no image."

Ben began to wonder if the man was playing a game, trying to scam him for money with a cock and bull story. But Andrew did sound genuinely frightened. And Ben had witnessed these spectres in the farmhouse himself.

"As I say, if I were you I'd abandon the place, otherwise your life might be at risk. I've come across strange apparitions, but the foreboding linked with these is something beyond anything I've experienced. Rest assured, I won't be billing you."

"I don't want to abandon the place," Ben was growing more frustrated at the prospect of losing the idyllic retirement farmhouse he'd planned for him and his wife.

"Then the only thing I can suggest is that you find a priest willing to carry out an exorcism," Andrew suggested. "But that's out of my province."

They finished their conversation and Ben remained sitting on the bed in his room considering the next move. He settled on the ghost hunter's suggestion of having the spirits exorcised. Perhaps the vicar at the local church of St Peter's on the brow of the hill behind the village could help. It was worth a try. Anything worth a try to overcome this paranormal horror.

Leaving aside work on the outbuildings for the time being, Ben made his way up the narrow lane leading to St Peter's church. He wondered if the vicar there might think him a bit odd seeking the services of an exorcism. It wasn't exactly common practise in the church any more, and mostly regarded as something belonging to a less enlightened past.

Ben lifted the black metal latch on the lychgate entrance into the grounds, and walked along the paved path cutting through the graveyard to the arched doorway of the centuries old church.

Inside, pews lined each side of the central aisle leading towards the altar. The vaulted church ceiling rose high above. Stained glass windows adorned the length of the building.

He saw a woman polishing a crucifix at the altar. She turned on hearing him approach, an inquisitive smile rising on her elderly face.

"I'm looking for the vicar?" he asked.

"You need to go to the vicarage," she replied. "Out of the door and take the path to the right."

Ben thanked her and left, taking the narrow gravel path towards the vicarage, an old greystone house a short distance ahead. As he neared, the front door opened and a woman wearing a surplice came out. Ben was greeted by another inquisitive smile, this time rising on a much younger woman's rosy face.

"I'm looking for the vicar," he repeated his quest.

"Then you've found her," she replied. "Reverend Angela Watson. But please call me Angela."

For a moment Ben was thrown. He'd expected the vicar to be a man, but it was no problem for him. Man or woman, it was help he needed.

He faltered, not knowing how to begin without sounding like a nut. The narrative of suffering hauntings suddenly seemed unreal away from the setting of the farmhouse.

"Something troubling you?" asked the vicar, seeing a perplexed expression on his face. Ben struggled to work his way into words.

"You'll probably think I'm mad, but I'm being haunted by ghosts," he began, expecting the reverend to eye him with disbelieving caution.

"Are you?" she replied, as if he'd said nothing out of the ordinary. "Walk with me. I'm going to check an old tree at the far end of the graveyard that looks in danger of collapsing on someone. We prefer people to be dead *before* they arrive here for burial."

The Rev Watson's humorous stab made him feel more relaxed. She hadn't immediately dismissed him as a crank. They walked on a grass pathway through the graveyard as Ben related his terrifying experiences at the farmhouse. How he was now looking for someone of holy orders to perform an exorcism.

"Yes, definitely needs some work doing on it," the vicar studied the old chestnut tree leaning over at a precarious angle at the far end of the graveyard. "Pity if we can't save it. Been here a long time."

Ben wondered if she'd listened to a word he'd said. The woman considered the plight of the tree for a little longer, then turned to him.

"I don't perform exorcisms," she told him. "I've heard all the rumours about the farmhouse and always taken it as country gossip. Old legends. But hearing it from you, an outsider, makes me wonder what is fact and what is fiction?" she paused.

"Of course, I don't know you, but it would be wrong for me to dismiss your story out of hand. The experience is obviously very real to you," the reverend was giving Ben's tale consideration.

He began to think she was verging into the patronising. Dismissing him in the guise of being understanding.

"I'm not sure that I believe in spirits rising from the dead as ghosts, other than our Holy Lord rising from the grave," she continued.

Now Ben was coming to the conclusion he was wasting his time with her and prepared to leave.

"But I don't know everything," she added. "There's a lot beyond my understanding."

Ben's annoyance evaporated. The vicar was listening. Taking him on board. She targeted him with a serious gaze.

"I don't perform exorcisms, but I can put you in touch with a priest who does. Would that help?"

From wanting to storm away in disgust, Ben now felt a strong urge to hug her in gratitude. But that would hardly be appropriate for a woman of the cloth. He opted for a grateful smile instead.

They returned to the vicarage where she gave him the phone number of Father Shannon O'Connor, a Roman Catholic priest at the church of St Joseph's in Millfield, a small town about thirty miles away. In thanks for the vicar's help, Ben offered to undertake any building work needed at her church for a much lower rate than she would find elsewhere. Both parties departed content with a positive out-come.

******

FATHER O'Connor sounded intrigued by Ben's story of the farmhouse hauntings.

"I haven't been asked to perform an exorcism for years," he replied to Ben's phone call, sounding as though he relished the opportunity. "I have a number of other engagements at the moment," he went on, "but I could come over in a couple of days."

A time for the priest's arrival was agreed.

With the prospect of no longer having to spend nights at the property, Ben was happy to wait. He could work on the outbuildings in the daytime, when the potential visitation of spirits seemed less daunting.

He returned to the farmstead from the village and began clearing rubble from an outbuilding where the old roof had entirely caved in. It was arduous work, and as he stooped over the pile of broken slates he was stacking outside, he became aware of something staring at him.

Standing up and turning, he saw a brown hawk curiously eyeing him. It was perched on the partly remaining tiled roof of an outbuilding on the opposite side of the track. As Ben stared back, the bird's gaze appeared to become almost defiant, as if challenging him. Ben wondered if it was one of the hawks that had visited him shortly after he'd arrived. The creature's gaze was strangely unnerving.

He clapped his hands to shoo it away. The bird maintained its defiance, refusing to budge. He was tempted to pick up a stone from the track and throw it at the creature, but resisted. One, he didn't wish to harm the hawk and two, he thought it ridiculous to be unsettled by a just a bird. He turned away to get on with his work, still sensing the creature staring at him.

Then he heard wings flapping as the hawk took off. He watched it flying down the track towards the field at the bottom and settling in the large oak tree on the other side of the wooden gate and fence.

For some inexplicable reason Ben felt an urge to walk to the end of the track following the direction of the bird. Most of the leaves had fallen from the oak and the hawk was visible perched high up. His attention was drawn to a sturdy branch lower down jutting sideways from the tree. It was about ten feet above the grass.

Now the words of the historian woman, Marian Armstrong, came to mind. The bit about the original owners of the farm John Trevallion and his wife being strung up from a tree. Was it this one? That overhanging branch could be roughly the right height to sling a noosed rope over. The vision of bodies hanging from it surfaced in his imagination.

The hawk continued to stare at him, craning its head from side to side. The bird shuffled along its high branch perch, then launched into the air, making a brief circle above Ben before flying away across the field into the distance.

He walked back along the track and continued working for a while. But he couldn't get that damnable bird out of his mind. For some reason he felt it carried some kind of portent. Something evil approaching.

He attempted to dismiss the thought. Perhaps his experiences at the farmhouse were beginning to influence his rational mind. There must be many hawks in this country area with not a thought in their heads beyond feeding and mating. But however much he tried to rationalise the bird's visit, he could not push away the feeling of impending horror.

Ben worked a little longer then decided to call it a day, looking forward to at least spending a peaceful night in his bed and breakfast lodging.

As he walked to his Transit van, he stopped to study a stone outbuilding. Its back wall was attached to the farmhouse lounge on the other side. Unlike the other outbuildings it was still intact with little deterioration.

So far, he hadn't looked inside the structure. There was no window and the heavy wooden door was locked. It had a large, old fashioned keyhole and would have been locked and unlocked with a sizable metal key. He concluded the only way in would be to force the door lock with a jemmy.

Something had kept puzzling him about the structure of this outbuilding, but right now it wasn't a high priority and he was tired. He set off for the village and the new lodging. His hope for a peaceful future now rested with Father O'Connor and the exorcism.

# CHAPTER 4

THE PRIEST called at the farmhouse late afternoon a couple of days later. His world weary face gave the appearance of a man who had shared the burden of many harrowing, heart-rending emotions with his flock over the years. His complexion was almost as white as his thinning hair, eyes and cheeks resting in hollows. Still he managed to retain a welcoming smile.

Ben came out to meet him as he lifted a black holdall from the boot of his elderly red Vauxhall Corsa car. The man looked reassuringly official wearing his priestly robes. After making coffee in the kitchen, Ben explained again the supernatural visits he'd suffered.

"Is there somewhere in the place where you feel the manifestations are at their strongest," Father O'Connor enquired.

"The lounge, definitely the lounge," Ben replied without hesitation.

They finished their coffees and went into the lounge, where the priest opened the holdall and began preparation for the exorcism ceremony.

He placed a silver crucifix in the centre of the mantelpiece above the brick fireplace, and lit two candles in silver holders at each end. He then lit an incense burner on a chain, which he asked Ben to hold for a moment while he removed a book from the holdall, turning the pages to the place he required.

Taking the open book in one hand and the incense burner in the other, he stood ready for the proceeding.

"There may be some strange manifestations," the priest warned Ben. "If you want to leave the room, I don't mind."

Ben was reluctant to experience more occult events. He'd put up with enough. But he also wanted to witness the dispelling of those unwelcome visitors from the other side.

"I'll stay," he replied, not sounding overly enthusiastic.

Father O'Connor faced the mantelpiece bearing the cross and candles and began swinging the incense burner, the sweet vapour starting to ooze through the room while he recited from the book. Ben stood a short distance away. The words being uttered sounded incomprehensible to him. Like a foreign language.

For several minutes nothing happened, then Ben became aware of a cool draft starting to sweep across the room. The door and lattice window were shut, leaving no natural reason for the air's entry. The priest continued to recite from the book, the disturbed air now beginning to affect the back and forth swing of the incense burner, causing it to move in a slightly circular motion.

Ben heard a growing sound of rumbling. The room began to shake. He instinctively wanted to flee, thinking an earthquake was taking place and the farmhouse was about to collapse, but he found himself unable to move.

Tormented screams of horror echoed through the room. He could see Father O'Connor starting to shudder uncontrollably as if his body was gripped by an invisible hand shaking him violently. The incense burner and book flew out of the priest's hands, hurtling to the floor. The crucifix on the mantelpiece rocked and toppled on to the hearth below, swiftly followed by the candles, their flames blown out in the erupting fury.

Father O'Connor's shaking grew more violent and suddenly an invisible force lifted him into the air, his arms and legs flailing helplessly. He cried out in agony, his voice joining the horrific screams from unseen souls filling the room.

Ben's jaw dropped in terror. He stood locked rigid unable to move. He wanted to grab the priest and bundle him out of the God forsaken room, but had no choice. Another invisible power was forcing him to remain in the surrounding evil.

Then the chaos subsided. The priest was dropped to the ground. Ben thought it was all over. Within seconds an immense pressure started to build, a crushing force closing in on their bodies, squeezing the air out of their lungs. The massive pressure made it impossible to breath. Soon both men started suffocating, staggering around nearing an agonising death.

As consciousness began to fade, the lattice window to the side furiously exploded into the room, showering them with vicious fragments of flying glass. The pressure subsided. They both began gasping for air.

A figure started to materialise from the wall where a few days earlier Ben had seen the apparition of the young woman enter the room. But this manifestation was the image of the man he'd also seen appear in the bedroom. Long straggly hair and glaring evil eyes in a deeply lined face. The man broke into a wicked, gloating laugh, relishing the delight of trapping a victim for the kill. Then he disappeared.

Father O'Connor swayed on his feet in a state of exhausted shock. He began to topple backwards and Ben rushed forward to stop his fall. The man was unconscious. He rested him on the floor and began to wonder if the priest was dead. His face appeared deathly white.

After a few moments Father O'Connor opened his eyes. They flickered from side to side looking confused. Consciousness flowed back and he quickly sat up, staring around at the fallen crucifix and candle holders, the room littered with broken glass. Slowly he stood up, every joint in his bones aching.

Ben saw fragments of glass embedded in the priest's cheek, trails of blood running from them. At that moment he suddenly began to feel pain in his own cheek and realised sharp shards were also lodged in his face from the blast of the shattered window. The drama until now had numbed all his other senses.

Father O'Connor appeared disorientated, unsteady on his feet. Ben guided him out of the room and on to a canvas chair in the kitchen. He removed the pieces of glass from the man's face and washed away the drying blood. Fortunately he'd brought a first aid kit and was able to provide dressings.

He made the priest a strong cup of tea and then set about removing glass pieces from his own face, wincing at the pain as he drew them out. Thankfully their clothing had saved them from suffering greater bodily injury. Tears and grazing, but nothing serious. Father O'Connor gradually recovered as he drank the tea.

"Get out of this place as soon as you can," were the first words he said to Ben. "Immediately I'd advise you. It is truly evil. Only deep love can lead the tormented spirits to rise against the horror. Until then, the hell that dwells here will remain."

Ben wanted him to say exactly what he meant, but the priest stood up and left for the lounge to collect the items he'd brought with him for the ceremony. Picking them up and placing them in the holdall he turned to Ben in the hallway, issuing a dire warning.

"I've exorcised spirits from many places over the years, but this one is an exception. I believe your life is in mortal danger if you remain here."

"What do you mean about only deep love rising against the horror...?" Ben didn't finish the sentence. Father O'Connor opened the front door.

"It's beyond your remit. It's beyond my remit. Just get out of here," the priest replied and left.

Ben stood at the open door watching the man place the holdall in the back of his car and driving away. His last hope of making the farmhouse a habitable setting for peaceful retirement had evaporated.

But dammit, he would not give in. The dead would have to be put in their place. His resolve faded a little when he re-entered the lounge to clear up the shattered glass spread around the room.

The memory of the horror grew vivid in his mind again and he constantly looked over his shoulder. The broken window would need covering with a sheet of wood, though that could wait until tomorrow. Now he wanted to just get away from the place. Surely someone, somewhere would be able to help him stop these terrifying hauntings.

******

ROSE Partridge, the landlady at Ben's bed and breakfast lodging, outwardly displayed more thorns than blooms. She may have been a sweet rose many years earlier, but life's hardships had etched a sour expression on her face. She seemed unable to raise a friendly smile in greeting or conversation.

Ben found her manner not aggressive, just dispassionate, and her thorns seemed to be more defensive than threatening. He guessed the woman must be in her mid-sixties, silver hair in tong curls and often wearing a frumpy, dark green cotton dress.

Despite all her keep away signs, she generously offered to cook him an evening meal when he returned, not keeping strictly to the terms of bed and breakfast.

"I've got no other guests this time of year," she croaked tersely, appearing in the gloomy brown hallway from the kitchen as Ben was about to go upstairs to his room. "So it'll be no trouble."

The invitation was more than he could have hoped for. He'd planned to go to the nearby cafe for a meal, but was exhausted and had begun considering not to bother.

"It'll only be chicken leg and some vegetables," Rose snapped uninvitingly.

"That would be fine," Ben replied.

"Ready in half-an-hour," she grunted and disappeared back to the kitchen.

After freshening up, Ben made his way to the small dining room downstairs. Five other tables remained bare, the sixth had a place mat set with knife and fork. A net curtain covered the front window overlooking the street and cottages opposite. A couple of prints depicting countryside views were hanging above a dresser bearing condiments on a tray.

Rose entered carrying a plate in one hand and a jug of gravy in the other, plonking them unstylishly on the table. The food looked dull and colourless, as if suffering itself from malnutrition. The trauma of Ben's weird exorcism terrors now robbed him of appetite. His forced desire to suppress the stress was beginning to seep out. But Rose was being kindly despite her sour nature. He pressed himself to eat. She returned to the dining room just as he was finishing the meal.

"Here on business?" she asked, sounding more like the demand for an answer than a request.

Ben told her he'd bought Fairview Farm and that he was here to carry out renovations on the outbuildings. The landlady's sour expression didn't change, but her eyes became thoughtful, as if the unfortunate legend about the farmstead was well known to her.

"Wouldn't bloody well go near the place myself," she delivered her opinion with no frills. "Dead Spirits Farm it's known as round here." Her opinion gave no comfort to her guest.

"So I've heard," he replied, while she began to clear the gravy jug and empty plate from the table. "I've got deep reservations about the place too."

"You've seen things?" Rose stopped, plate and jug suspended in her hands.

"I've seen things, as you put it," Ben said wearily. He started to feel unburdened, leaning towards seeing her as a mother confessor. She would not carry the weight of worry and emotion that would burden his wife Eleanor with the knowledge.

"I'll make you a cup of tea," Rose replied, her thorns beginning to retract and the petals starting to sympathetically bloom.

A few minutes later she returned with tea for both of them and sat down at the table with Ben. He recounted the story of his plans for the farmhouse and the terror now standing in his way. The sourness in Rose's face began to soften, a warmer nature surfacing.

"Well I know it must be hard for you. Making those plans for you and your wife. But that bloody place is evil. You'll have to make a choice between losing money on it or losing your sanity," she paused, "or maybe even worse."

"What do you mean?" Ben wondered what she meant by those last words.

"People have disappeared there in the past. Nothing to say it can't happen again even now. Get out for your own sake and your wife's." Rose could see he was reluctant to give up his quest.

"I was married for years," Rose reflected, "but my husband couldn't keep his cock in his pants. Always off with other women. Kept breaking my heart. I stuck it out for the sake of our two daughters. When they were old enough, I threw him out." The woman's eyes deepened with the hurtful memory.

"My daughters thought I was terrible. I'd always hidden his ways from them. For my pains, they cut me off. Haven't seen or heard from them in twenty years."

For a moment Ben entirely forgot his own troubles. Now he began to understand the frosty nature of the woman sitting with him.

"Sometimes you have to put up with the shitty decisions you make in life," Rose concluded. "Right now you've got the opportunity to change things. I haven't."

Both were thoughtfully silent for a moment. Then Rose stood up.

"Anyway, I've got clearing up to do," her defensive mood returned.

"Yes, and I'm going to get an early night," Ben smiled. "Just hope I can get to sleep. Never felt unnerved like this before."

Rose didn't return the smile, but her barrier had given way a little.

\*\*\*\*\*\*

BEN returned to the farmhouse next morning. He hadn't slept well and had seriously considered Rose Partridge's advice. But obstinacy and never falling at hurdles had been his recipe for success in business life. If anything, his deter-mination to beat those ghouls standing in his way grew even stronger. Someone had to put an end to it.

His first job was to board up the smashed lounge win-dow overlooking the forecourt at the front. He carried wooden boards in the van and spent the next hour fixing one to the opening.

While working on the boarding his mind kept wandering to the hauntings. The apparitions seemed to be centered on the sidewall in the lounge. The wall attached to the locked outbuilding at the side. Perhaps an answer to the visitations lay inside it. There was no key so he'd have to break in.

After boarding the window he collected a drill from the Transit van and prepared to drill out the rusted keyhole mechanism to get inside. Raising the drill to begin, he no-ticed a rusty key laying beside the outbuilding wall a few feet away. A large key. One that looked like it would fit the lock.

Ben thought it odd that the key could have laid there for so long without anyone noticing it. Maybe it had been buried under soil which had gradually been washed away by rain. Or had some other power placed it there for him?

He slotted it into the keyhole. It fitted. The rust on both key and inside the lock made it awkward to turn and took several attempts before giving way. The door was stiffly jammed against the frame. Ben had to give it a shoulder barge before it grudgingly opened.

If he'd been expecting an immediate answer to the mys-tery of the hauntings, the inside did not yield a clue. The outbuilding was empty. The ceiling and walls covered in thick cobwebs. Dust and dirt spread over the stone slab floor. A musty smell of damp and mould.

His heart sank. He'd pinned hopes on finding a solution inside to the problem. Had even harboured the thought of perhaps discovering a skeleton of some wretch whose spirit haunted the place and wouldn't rest until given a proper burial. A fanciful idea he knew. Desperation was leading him to imagine all sorts of possibilities that could provide an answer.

Ben locked the door and placed the key in the Transit van, then halfheartedly returned to carrying out more work on the other outbuildings. But his enthusiasm was starting to fade. Maybe he should take Rose Partridge's advice, as well as the priest's and the ghosthunter's to get out. Until now he'd maintained his enthusiasm for the farmhouse to Eleanor in phone calls. Perhaps the time had come for him to tell her the truth.

Driving back later to his lodging in the village, something nagged at his mind about the empty outbuilding. He just couldn't work out what it was. He'd missed something. The harder he tried to figure out the puzzle the more the answer evaded him.

As he entered the hallway at Rose's cottage, he could hear her talking to a man in the kitchen. Rose had heard Ben enter and came out to greet him.

"Glad you're safely back from that place," she said. The man in the kitchen emerged from behind her, his face full of healthy colour under a crop of curly fair hair. Ben estimated the visitor to be in his mid-thirties.

"This is Jason Coleman," Rose introduced the man, "he owns Millhouse Farm. which is the next one from yours."

Jason stepped forward, forearm muscles bulging from his short sleeve blue shirt, mud stains streaking his black jeans.

"Been meaning to call round on you," he thrust out his hand to shake Ben's. "But been so busy at my farm until now. Rose told me you were staying here, so I came round to catch you coming in."

"Let's all have a cup of tea," Rose invited.

"Another time if that's okay," Jason made his apology. "I've got the vet coming out shortly to look at a cow that isn't doing so well."

Rose seemed disappointed.

Jason turned to Ben.

"What I wanted to ask is if you'd like to come over to The Wheatsheaf pub in the high street tonight? Meet some of the locals? Have a game of darts?"

The plan Ben had in mind was to get some rest. But perhaps the invitation was just what he needed. Something to take his mind off things for a while.

"Okay, I'd enjoy that," he replied.

He couldn't know fate was closing in on him. It was a wise choice to make the most of some entertainment while it was still available.

******

THE Wheatsheaf pub was packed with locals from the village and surrounding areas, mostly farm workers drinking at the bar and talking together in groups with pints of beer in hand.

Ben felt a complete stranger as he entered the premises. Dark wood ceiling beams bowing in the middle, and the slightly uneven stone slab floor indicating the pub's grand age stretching back a couple of hundred years or more.

Faces turned towards him as he began to move between the crowd, curious eyes wondering who was this unknown visitor at the locals' social night. Ben started to feel distinctly out of place, then Jason talking to friends at the bar spied him.

"Ben!" he called, cutting into the noisy conversations filling the room. "Come and have a drink. What's your poison?" He shook Ben's hand and ordered him a pint of beer. Jason introduced the newcomer to the group of farmer friends with him, bosses and farm workers putting aside rank for their social gathering.

"This is the new owner of Fairview Farm," he said. For a second a glint of amazement flickered in the men's eyes. It was obvious they were well versed in the legend of the farm and considered anyone wanting to live there to be insane. But the reaction passed and they returned smiles of greeting.

"What made you buy the place?" one of the men asked, as Jason handed Ben his pint of beer.

"It's my plan to settle there with my wife for a peaceful early retirement," Ben replied.

Again eyes briefly filled with incredulity, though no-one it seemed on this social occasion wanted to spoil the atmosphere with tales of dread about the farm. Ben could see what was going on in their minds.

"Okay gents," a man boomed above the noise of the bar, "it's time for the darts match."

"Yeah!" cries rang out from the crowd.

"And tonight we'll see if Croft Farm can retain the title, or if their strong challenger Millhouse Farm can thrash the daylights out of them," the announcer wound the atmosphere. Cheers and boos filled the air.

"I hope you're good at darts," Jason smiled at Ben, "because tonight you are my honorary Millhouse Farm team member."

The elevation to an important role took Ben by surprise. He thought it would be a relaxed game of darts. Now reputation was riding on him.

"Sorry to spring it on you, but Rose tells me you've had a rough time. This'll get your mind off it for a while," Jason winked.

For the next hour the teams battled it out. Ben had played the game in earlier years, and although not expert, played well. When Jason's Millhouse Farm team wrested victory from the previous champions, ecstatic joy broke out among the winners.

"Well done," Jason praised his new player. "You'll have to play for our team again."

The evening and triumph had certainly relieved Ben's mind for a while. As the atmosphere settled, they sat together at a table.

"I don't want to put a downer on things," Jason began reluctantly, "but you'd be better off getting out of that farm. No-one round here would touch it with a barge pole."

The man's advice was not new to Ben and he was grateful that people had his welfare at heart. However, it wasn't easy just to walk away from his dream, his plan for the future.

"I appreciate what you're saying," he replied after considering Jason's warning, "but there has to be a way of making the place normal again."

"Various owners have thought that for a couple of centuries. The last people who bought it renovated the place, but didn't stay long because of strange happenings there," Jason explained. It was news to Ben. The estate agent Justin Turnbull had obviously kept that bit of vital information from him.

Jason sensed the newcomer to the village was determined to defy the light of experience, so he decided to drop the subject not wanting to dampen the happier surroundings any further.

After a couple more pints of ale and chatting to the locals, Ben returned to his lodging just a short walk away feeling relaxed. For now the evening's distraction and the beer helped to block the stresses of the last few days.

However, even away from the terrors of the farmhouse, his sleep became haunted with visions of spectres and people warning him to leave the place.

He woke in a cold sweat hearing knocking at the door. For a moment in the darkness he thought he was back at the farmhouse with a ghostly presence arising.

"Are you alright?" he heard the familiar voice of Rose calling to him at the door. "I heard you crying out."

Relief surged through him, swiftly followed by embarrassment. He felt a fool at disturbing her, unaware that his nightmarish dreams had broken into cries.

"I'm fine. Must have been a bad dream," he attempted to play it down.

"Just as long as you're alright," Rose replied sympathetically.

"Yes, I'm okay."

Ben laid awake for some time, fearful of returning to sleep and being haunted by the dreams, as well as not wishing to be embarrassed again. As he rested in bed, something else must have been puzzling his subconscious alongside the ghosts and dire warnings. Suddenly it surfaced.

The old outbuilding attached on the other side of the lounge wall. Now it came to him the inside of that structure seemed smaller than the outside length. Why? That didn't make sense.

As he recalled the image of the inside, it also came to him that a section of wall at one end had been built with a different type of stone. Smaller in size and not as grey looking as the rest of the walls. The cobwebs, dirt and dust had obscured immediate recognition.

Was it a false wall? And if so, why? Was the secret of the supernatural disturbances hidden there? Ben decided further investigation was necessary.

\*\*\*\*\*\*

ROSE was proud of cooking her guests a full English breakfast. Eggs, bacon, sausages, tomatoes, mushrooms, hash browns, baked beans and fried bread. But that morning Ben had no appetite for the day's starter meal. His landlady's face sunk into disappointment when he opted just to have cereal and a pot of tea.

"You look very pasty. That farmhouse is doing you no good," she admonished him with a frown steeped in concern. "Why don't you just get rid of it and find a nice cottage in the area if you want to live here."

Ben was seriously considering the idea. The locals he'd met had seemed a friendly enough bunch. But today he planned to check that outbuilding. He was thankful Rose hadn't mentioned the incident in the night. He could see now she had all the outward appearance of a hard woman, while inside carried a caring heart.

It was ridiculous, but Ben suddenly felt tearful, as if this was the last time he'd ever see the woman. That he would never see his wife or children again. This was insane, the whole business was leading him towards a nervous breakdown.

In that moment he decided enough is enough. He would abandon the plan to live at the farmhouse no matter what the financial loss. It would probably take years to find another person wanting to buy the property.

Maybe his only option would be to give it away. Let ghost hunters use it for research. Or else just demolish the place. Blast it into outer space. Reason was beginning to leave him. But first he intended to see if anything lay behind that inside stonework he'd now convinced himself was a false wall. Then the farmhouse could go to hell.

\*\*\*\*\*\*

BEN parked his van on the track beside the outbuilding. To be certain of his conclusion on the different sizes of the structure, he first measured the inside length and then the outside.

He was right. There was a three foot difference indicating the high possibility of a false wall. Demolishing the wall with a sledgehammer would be the best way to break through.

As he went back to the van to fetch the sledgehammer, he caught sight of a hawk perched on top of the outbuilding's slate roof.

The bird stared at him, eyes gazing sternly, seeming to know what he was planning. Could it be the same hawk that had studied him a couple of days earlier when it was perched on one of the other outbuildings? The creature again had the effect of unsettling him. Maybe he was reading too much into just a bird.

The hawk clawed itself sideways along the rooftop then took off, swooping round the track before directly aiming at Ben with its vicious beak poised to attack. He ducked, feeling the breeze as its wings swept past within a hair's breadth of striking his head.

Ben sprung up to see it flying down the track and settling on the oak tree branch in the field at the far end. That outstretched branch where he thought John Trevallion and his wife might have been hanged.

Normally he would have considered a bird attack on a human unusual, but not indicative of anything supernatural. Now he began to wonder if the creature possessed some evil presence.

Putting the thought aside, he pressed on with his mission to demolish the false wall. The cement holding it in place was old and crumbling, but not so weak for it to take half-an-hour of sledgehammering to break through a few of the stone blocks it secured.

A strong breeze started to blow outside, causing the out-building door to swing open and shut on its rusty hinges. Ben returned to the Transit van to fetch a torch and shine it into the small cavity he'd created, but the opening wasn't yet wide enough to get a good view of the inside.

As he delivered more blows with the sledgehammer, the outbuilding door continued opening and shutting in the breeze and began to annoy him. There was no latch or catch on the door so he locked it shut with the key, continuing the work by torchlight.

With more stonework gradually giving way, he could now reach in with the torch and inspect inside. To the farm-track side of the structure it was just original wall. To the lounge wall side, he could see a door. A heavy wooden door.

A few more blows and soon there was enough space for him to enter the cavity. He laid the sledgehammer on the floor and stepped inside. Sealed off for so many years, the narrow enclosure was musty damp. He examined the door in the torchlight and could see it had a large keyhole lock, but no key in it. This would also need a sledgehammer blow to force entry.

Stepping outside to pick up the implement, he heard what he thought was the sound of a key turning in the lock. As he entered again, the door was now half open. Was there someone behind it? Impossible surely? Ben felt the hair on the back of his head bristle. Was this the work of another ungodly agent wandering the property?

Torn between getting out and curiosity to see what lay behind the door, curiosity won. He shoved it fully open and shone the torch into the darkness. The beam located a stone stairway leading beneath the farmhouse lounge.

Cautiously he began to descend the steps into a cellar. Not for the first time in this hellish place his heart began to pound as the torchlight picked out a stone slab floor at the bottom. He stepped on to it and shone the light around. At first it appeared the cellar was empty, just dusty cobwebbed walls on all sides. Then he highlighted a scene of jaw dropping horror.

Scattered in a huge heap against the far wall, fragmented pieces of arm and leg bones came into view, rib cages and skulls. Unceremoniously discarded like junk.

Ben staggered back at the terrible sight. What the hell had happened here? As he fought to resist spewing out his guts, the cellar began to glow in a dim blue light.

"Welcome," a man's voice came from behind. Ben turned. The horror was not yet over.

# CHAPTER 5

ELEANOR was growing increasingly worried. Her husband Ben hadn't called her for three days. Normally she would receive a daily call when he travelled into the village to contact her.

At first she thought he might have been too busy to make the drive and was perfectly okay. But three days silence? Now it was becoming unusual.

Back at the office she told Ken Wainwright about her worries. He was a short, stocky man, now in middle age with thinning peppery hair, but still retaining his wide, bull like physique. It had served to keep some of the rougher construction workers in their place when he was site foreman for the company in earlier years.

Now he organised projects from the office, occasionally visiting sites to ensure discipline remained the law. Eleanor trusted him absolutely. Totally loyal.

"I need to go and see if Ben's alright," she explained to Ken's concerned look.

"I'll come with you," he grunted in his normal curt delivery.

"No, it's okay. Ben's probably fine. But if you can keep an eye on things here, that will be a great help," Eleanor smiled.

"Of course," Ken's return of a smile was hard work for him. He didn't do it very often. Eleanor knew he had a soft heart somewhere inside him, though he never wanted to display it to the world. He was content to live a life alone in his flat down the road.

She packed a few things and set off on the long drive to the farmhouse. Although worried, she fully expected to see her husband busy at work on the outbuildings. Or perhaps he was enjoying a bit of me time away from her for a while. As she drove there, she considered several ways to give him a good dressing down for ignoring her.

Pulling up on the farmhouse forecourt, Eleanor left the car and approached the front door. Ben's Transit van wasn't parked outside and she wondered if he was out somewhere. She didn't have a front door key so she'd probably have to wait until he returned. She tried the handle anyway. The door opened.

"Ben," she called from the hallway, "it's Eleanor." Her call was met by silence. She looked in the kitchen, the living room with its trestle table and canvas chairs, then the lounge. The window had been boarded up. Ben must have been doing some work on it.

Realising her husband wasn't present inside the property, she decided to look outside, walking round the side to the stony track. The Transit van came into view. The back doors were open. Ben was at work somewhere nearby, she sighed with relief preparing to give him a mouthful for not keeping in touch.

"Ben," she called again. Still no reply. Maybe he was in the outbuilding that the van was parked beside. She pushed at the door, but it was locked.

Deciding he must be further down the track, she walked past the derelict outbuildings noting the piles of rubble that Ben had assembled for later collection. Then she noticed a hawk perched on top of a stone wall that bordered a roofless building. The bird stared at her inquisitively. It made Eleanor feel uncomfortable. She liked birds, but this one seemed strangely different. There was no rhyme or reason why. She turned away ignoring it. Where was Ben? That was the pressing question.

She called out to him again. Still no reply. Perhaps he was out walking somewhere. Eleanor went to the bottom of the track, stopping at the wooden gate leading into the field.

She heard wings flapping overhead. The hawk soared above and settled on the large outstretched branch of the oak tree. Ideal for slinging a noosed rope over. Not that the thought entered Eleanor's mind. She was unaware of local legends. Ben had protected her from country talk.

She turned her back on the bird and returned to the farmhouse deciding to wait for him wherever he was. In the kitchen she filled the kettle to make a coffee then saw a bottle of milk on the counter which appeared discoloured. A mouldy growth inside. Ben couldn't have been in here for a couple of days or more. He was inclined not to fuss too much about food that might be slightly out of date, but even he wouldn't keep putrid milk. Where was he?

Now Eleanor began to grow seriously worried. Had he decided to desert her? Did he have a secret lover? Was the new home in the country a ploy to escape her? Run off with someone else? Eleanor couldn't avoid the thoughts, but she knew that was not her Ben.

He had a roving eye sometimes. That was men. Her husband had always been totally faithful. She knew the guilt would break him if he ever exercised his fantasies with anyone else.

No. Something was wrong.

Should she call the police? It was probably too soon for that. There was nothing suspicious that anyone other than her would take seriously yet.

Eleanor had a sleeping bag in the car and had planned to spend a night or so at the farmhouse. She and Ben had roughed it together on building sites in portakabins and sheds in their younger days setting up the business. She'd imagined reliving some of those times with him. But what now?

It had been a long drive to the property and the early winter sun was dipping close to the horizon. Ben would be back for sure. In the meantime she settled in the farmhouse. Eleanor knew there was no phone signal or internet connection, but she'd brought a couple of books for entertainment in the quieter periods.

The sunlight disappeared and darkness filled the window as she sat on a canvas chair in the living room with a cup of black coffee. The thriller she was reading had taken her mind off matters for a while, but her attention started to stray as she began to wonder why Ben still hadn't returned. It was frustrating not being able to contact him by phone.

Eleanor concluded she'd have to spend the night in the property alone. There was probably a perfectly rational reason for his absence. And, of course, with no signal here, even if he was trying to contact her it wouldn't get through.

Darker thoughts began to surface in her mind as the evening slipped into late night. If he hadn't returned by morning she'd go into the village to contact the police. Find out if they may have heard something.

Eleanor decided to set up her sleeping bag in the bedroom upstairs beside Ben's unoccupied bag. At least she would be near him in spirit. A good night's sleep and it would all turn out right in the morning she thought. She smiled remembering that was her mother's catchphrase when Eleanor had been upset in childhood.

She undressed and prepared to climb into the sleeping bag when the room light began to flicker, going out for a few seconds. The brief darkness was unsettling. She didn't have a torch and the moment seemed to bestow the atmosphere of an unseen presence. Being watched.

"Don't be ridiculous," she said to herself out loud, feeling stupid to be rattled by what was an obvious short interruption to the power supply. Still, something inside urged her to be aware. On guard. Ben had never mentioned anything strange about the farmhouse. No, it's just being alone in an unfamiliar place, Eleanor reasoned against her instincts. But she'd leave the light on for the night. She settled in the sleeping bag, and after wondering for a while where Ben might be, she gradually fell asleep.

The bedroom was in darkness when she opened her eyes. She could hear voices downstairs. Had Ben returned with some other people? Been out on the binge? Why was the room light off? She sat bolt upright then climbed out of the sleeping bag fumbling in the darkness to where the door approximately stood. She felt the handle and pulled it down.

"Ben!" her voice echoed along the landing and down the stairs into the hallway. The call received absolute silence.

"Who's there?" Eleanor began to panic. Were they thieves? Would they harm her? The landing light flickered on. She couldn't see anyone in the hallway below. She cautiously descended the stairs.

"Ben?" she called again. No reply. Eleanor nervously looked into the rooms. There was no-one present.

"There must have been another power cut. I must have imagined the voices in my sleep," she reasoned to herself out loud again, taking comfort from hearing a familiar voice, even if it was just her own. Further sleep was out of the question. She made herself a coffee in the kitchen and then went back upstairs to wash and put on a red T-shirt and black chinos.

Had something happened here to make Ben leave? The thought crossed her mind. No, he'd have told her.

Although she put the voices she'd heard in the night down to sleep imagination, Eleanor was rapidly coming to the conclusion she didn't want to spend another night here alone. She would tell Ben this was not the place for them. She didn't want to disappoint him, but sensed the farmhouse was not normal. He'd probably explode at her, but would eventually settle to the wish that made her happy. She loved him for that devotion to her.

Eleanor spent the rest of the night resting on the canvas chair in the kitchen. It seemed the only room that didn't have an uninviting feel.

When daylight broke she drove into the village, searching from her car along the high street for sight of the local police station. It didn't have one. She wasn't surprised, so many of them had been closed in cost saving measures.

She parked, and realising she now had a phone signal called Ben's number. It rang then switched to messaging. She left a message asking him to call back quickly.

After waiting fifteen minutes and receiving no reply, Eleanor decided to ring the police. The woman who answered wasn't entirely helpful.

"Your husband's a missing adult, so I suggest you wait a little longer," came the advice. Eleanor wasn't happy with that. She was growing concerned for Ben's safety and asked if any accidents had been reported locally.

"No," the woman replied after checking the log. "I can send round an officer covering that area, but it'll probably be a couple of hours," the woman on the line conceded in a tone that implied Eleanor was wasting police time. She accepted the offer.

While in the village Eleanor decided to go into the grocery store to buy some milk. At least she could have a fresh supply for her coffee while waiting for the officer to arrive.

"Passing through or staying for a visit?" asked the cheery woman serving behind the counter. Eleanor explained that she owned Fairview Farm and had come to join her husband there.

"Oh, I met him. Lovely man," the store owner's face filled with a smile.

"Trouble is, I can't seem to find him," Eleanor felt silly saying she'd lost her husband. She explained he hadn't been in touch for several days.

"No, I haven't seen him round here for a while," the woman replied, her smile now dropping into a frown. "I hope he's alright."

The woman's remark alarmed Eleanor.

"What do you mean?"

The shop owner appeared reluctant to answer. After a few moments she decided to voice her thoughts.

"Well the place has a bit of a history."

"History? What history?"

Again the woman hesitated to say more. She could see her customer had turned pale.

"It's..." she faltered, her voice lowering, "it's got a history of being haunted. Bad spirits."

Eleanor didn't know whether to laugh or take the words seriously. Out of the way village people, she thought, could always tell ludicrous tales, legends of ghosts and spirits that haunted old places. But Ben was missing. She had to consider all possibilities, although supernatural wasn't exactly high on her list.

The shopkeeper could see Eleanor's doubt.

"Well no-one knows for sure, but there's a highly educated lady lives here who can tell you about Fairview Farm," the shopkeeper explained, and gave Eleanor the address of Marian Armstrong, the same woman she'd directed Ben to visit.

Leaving the shop, it dawned on Eleanor the possible real reason why the farmhouse had been on sale so cheaply. It had a reputation of being haunted. She'd experienced the flickering lights, the power cut and the voices. Of course, those all came within the realm of natural possibility. She didn't like the atmosphere of the place, though that couldn't prove a supernatural presence.

Learning more about the history of the farm did intrigue Eleanor, and she planned to meet this Marian Armstrong. For now though finding Ben was the imperative. She drove back to the farmhouse to wait for the police officer's visit.

It was three hours before a police car drew up on the forecourt. A young man in uniform stepped out of the vehicle as she came up to greet him. The officer listened with keen interest to her concern. Then he took a look round the farmhouse and in the outbuildings along the track where Ben had been working, just in case he may have collapsed in some corner behind rubble and been overlooked. The locked outbuilding attached to the farm was the only place he didn't search.

"Doesn't look as though that key lock has been turned and opened for years," he concluded, looking at the faded wood surround and signs of rust in the mechanism. "Shouldn't think your husband's in there."

Eleanor was of the same opinion. Why would he lock himself away from the world in there? And if he was trapped inside, he would surely be hammering to be released on hearing sound and movement outside?

Then the officer asked if she and Ben had argued. The inquiry annoyed Eleanor.

"Of course we've had arguments," she responded sharply, "we've been married for years. But he's never gone missing as a result."

The officer looked apologetic, even though he felt it was necessary to ask. For now there was nothing else he could do. Ben was an adult, and unless there was a compelling suspicious circumstance, a full manhunt couldn't be launched unlike for a child.

"Give it another day or two," he advised. "If he hasn't returned by then, give us another call." He smiled sympathetically at Eleanor and left.

Now she felt entirely abandoned. Ben was her rock. Never far away. Steadfast. She needed so much for him to comfort and reassure her. She had a dread that something terrible had happened to him. In his absence she now longed to have her son and daughter by her side, but Michael was in Australia and Sophie a long distance away in the north. Should she call them? No. They'd be alarmed.

The police officer was probably right. Ben would turn up again. She'd stay in the area for a few days. Positive thinking calmed her. In the meantime she would visit the history woman recommended by the grocery store owner.

As Eleanor walked towards her car to drive into the village, she saw two hawks perched on the farmhouse roof staring down at her. Nothing unusual about that, except their presence felt unsettling. She looked away and got into the car, driving off with a sense of relief at leaving the property.

Marian Armstrong warmly welcomed Eleanor when she introduced herself as the new owner of Fairview Farm.

"Oh, your husband was here only a day or so ago, lovely man," Marian described him. Eleanor was pleased. Ben had made an obvious good impression on the locals, but she was puzzled as to why he had visited her. She asked.

"He told me he'd experienced some strange happenings there, visitations," the woman explained. The news worried Eleanor. She was invited into the drab living room where Marian recounted the legend of Fairview Farm, or its local name, Dead Spirits Farm. Now Eleanor became increasingly alarmed.

"Perhaps your husband's gone into Welford to order some building materials. It's our nearest town about twenty miles away," Marian offered words of comfort. "It's a beautiful area round there and he may have decided to stay in a guest house for a night or two."

Eleanor smiled at the comforting suggestion, but knew Ben would have called by now to say what he was doing. She thanked the woman for seeing her then returned to the car, sitting in it for a while to mull over the story of the farmhouse. Her rational mind told her hauntings were nonsense, but Ben it appeared had experienced something out of the ordinary. He wasn't one to run away with imaginings.

Should she spend another night at the farmhouse? If Ben turned up at least she'd be there. However, a bit of company wouldn't go amiss. She rang Ken Wainwright, the office manager back home, and told him Ben was still missing, and she'd appreciate him coming to join her for reasons of security.

Ken had no family or other commitments. Work was his life and he agreed immediately. After appointing someone to deputise for him he left for the farmhouse.

Eleanor returned to wait for him, hoping in the meantime Ben might have come back. He hadn't. What puzzled her was the Transit van still parked on the side track. Surely Ben would have used it to travel out somewhere? Maybe he'd taken a cab? That seemed unlikely, but perhaps she could enquire when she returned to the village tomorrow if any local cab drivers had been hired by him.

While waiting for Ken Wainwright to arrive, she decided to take another walk down the side track of the property.

The weather was unseasonably mild for the late season. Rich green pastures surrounding the farmstead and distant hills beyond made it an idyllic setting for her and Ben to settle down here she thought. She was certain when Ben returned they'd somehow be able to laugh off all this business of the supernatural.

Reaching the bottom of the track she saw two hawks perched on the outstretched branch of the old oak tree. They glared at her as if she was an intruder in their space. Eleanor suddenly felt annoyed by their stare. Ridiculous to feel intimidated by two birds.

"Shoo!" she waved her arms to scare them away. The creatures remained unmoved. Resolutely defiant. After a few more moments they launched into the air and aimed straight at her.

Eleanor ducked, feeling wings briefly beating her head as they swooped across. When she cautiously looked up again, the hawks were soaring away skyward across the field.

Now the birds were not just unsettling, but aggressively terrifying. Eleanor began to feel extremely vulnerable. Defending herself from any further aerial attack in the open would not be easy. She didn't have a shotgun, and anyway they could swoop silently from behind before she had a chance to react. And their long pointed beaks were vicious.

Her stroll down the track and rising hope that all would be well had been knocked sideways. As she began making her way back up the track, she caught sight of several men gathered outside the locked outbuilding. They looked rough, unshaven, wearing torn clothes. Were they thieves, or tramps here to take over the farmhouse for somewhere to live? She stopped, fearing for her safety.

The men appeared to have been talking to each other, now they turned to stare at her. Eleanor began backing away. Suddenly, instinct told her something was approaching from the air behind. She turned to see the hawks gliding over her. As she twisted back to see them flying on, her eyes flicked to ground level again. The group of men had disappeared. Had they gone round to the front the property? Warily she made her way to the front door. There was no-one about. Silence ruled.

Eleanor carefully searched each room, upstairs and down. No-one present. Perhaps the men were local farm people working nearby who'd met up there for a chat not realising the farmstead was still unoccupied.

In her heart of hearts she knew that was unlikely. Now she recalled the history woman, Marian Armstrong, telling her about long ago farm owner, John Trevallion, employing poor vagrants. About his cruelty, and how the vagrants seemed to mysteriously disappear. Perhaps murdered. But no, that couldn't have been their spirits she'd seen. That was ridiculous. Eleanor worked hard to push the thought out of her head. If she believed that, the only option would be to run screaming from the place.

# CHAPTER 6

ELEANOR was immensely relieved to hear Ken's car pulling up on the forecourt, and seeing the car headlights from the living room window cutting through the veil of surrounding darkness. As he stepped inside clutching a holdall, he could see the change in her.

Usually bright-eyed and full of enthusiasm, she now appeared pale and tired. She hugged him, thanking him for coming and apologising for causing the man inconvenience.

"You and Ben have been loyal and good to me over the years," he said, "I wouldn't dream of not helping." Ken dismissed Eleanor's need to apologise.

While she prepared a meal of sausages and mash for him, he unpacked a few things in the second bedroom upstairs.

"There must be a reason for Ben to be away," Ken attempted to comfort her as they sat eating at the table in the living room.

"He's never been out of contact this long," she replied, pouring out her concern.

"I've no doubt he'll return," Ken smiled. It didn't do anything to raise Eleanor's hopes. She prodded listlessly at her meal with the fork, unable to eat much. For a while they chatted about the early days of the building company, remembering some funny moments. That raised her spirit a little. Normally Ken's outer shell was always in place. Now she could see his softer inside as he did his best to keep her from sinking into depression.

Eleanor explained to him that the farmhouse had a local reputation for being haunted. That she'd felt unsettled by flickering lights, a power cut and hearing voices in the night. She'd gathered from Marian Armstrong that Ben had told her of strange happenings in the place.

Ken's expression indicated that he wasn't overly taken by supernatural explanations to unusual events.

"There's generally some rational reason for things we don't understand," he said. "Imagine what someone in the 17th century would make of a mobile phone. They'd think it was magic. Possibly even black magic being able to talk to someone miles away on some strange hand held device."

Eleanor couldn't disagree. Maybe there was a perfectly straightforward explanation for the foreboding atmosphere of the farmstead. But that didn't make her feel any less worried or more secure.

At eleven they decided it was time to get a night's rest. In the morning if Ben hadn't returned, she'd have to make a decision over the way forward.

Ken settled in his sleeping bag in the second bedroom and soon fell asleep. He awoke wondering if he'd been dreaming that voices were coming from downstairs. The air was silent, bright stars lit the window lending soft, shadowy light to the room. He must have been dreaming. Settling again, the silence was suddenly broken by the sound of a woman humming a tune. Was it Eleanor?

He climbed out the sleeping bag and switched on the light. Glancing at his watch he saw it was two-thirty in the morning. Surely Eleanor wouldn't be downstairs humming a tune at this time? Nor likely an intruder.

Quickly putting on his shirt and trousers, he opened the bedroom door on to the landing where the light had been left on. Cautiously he descended the stairs to the hallway. The living room door was half open, a dimmer light coming from inside. Was Eleanor in there? He approached and pushed the door wide open.

An oil lamp on a wooden table lit the room. A log fire burned in fireplace. To the side a china jug and bowl sat on a white lace cover spread across a dresser. Along the opposite wall a long, wooden bench held crockery, pots and utensils.

For a second Ken thought he might have been sleepwalking and ended up in a different property. No, that was impossible. The landing, stairs and hallway were familiar. But the living room, where he'd been only hours before, now looked as though it was from a different century. What was going on?

He heard a woman humming a tune approaching from the hallway. She entered and seeing him stopped. The young woman's brown hair was tied back in a bun. She wore a long, dark green dress and frowned at him from her chubby, round face.

"Farm workers are not allowed in Mr Trevallion's quarters," she admonished him. Ken stood staring at her totally stunned as she crossed the room and lifted a log from a pile stacked on the flagstone floor beside the fireplace, nimbly tossing it on the fire.

"That should keep it going for a while longer," she remarked to herself, then turned to Ken.

Much as he wanted to question her, he found himself completely transfixed by the apparition, unable to speak. The woman approached whispering to him.

"If I were you I'd leave this place. Mr Trevallion is giving you work, but you'll pay dearly for it. You're not safe here." The woman walked towards the door and left the room.

Ken's ability to move was swiftly restored. He had to catch up and speak to her. As he rushed towards her in the hallway, she faded into thin air.

He stood there, unable to process what he'd seen. Defying all the logic held in his head, gradually he began to accept the reality that he had seen a ghost. But the living room? Surely a room can't transform like that into an entirely different setting without a lot of noisy upheaval? He'd have heard it.

Ken returned to the room to take a look, switching on the light. The layout was exactly as it had appeared when he and Eleanor had retired to their bedrooms. The trestle table and canvas chairs. There was the fireplace and some of the original brickwork surround which had been retained by the previous owner, but no log fire burning, no wooden table or oil lamp, dresser or bench with utensils, pots and crockery. Ken was coming to the realisation that was how the room may have looked a hundred years or more ago. Was the woman he'd seen a ghost of that time?

"Is there something wrong?" Eleanor's voice from behind made him jump. She stood at the open doorway in her dressing gown. Ken struggled to reply for a second.

"Has something happened?" she could see his face was pale.

"I think I've seen a ghost," he finally managed to murmur.

Eleanor had never seen the man look so rattled. His usual manner of self-confidence and certainty shattered.

"What's happened?" she insisted, now growing deeply concerned.

"I could do with a drink," Ken replied.

"I think Ben brought some beers along with him. Come to the kitchen. Tell me what happened."

He followed her into the kitchen where Eleanor found a can of beer in the cupboard. She waited until he'd taken a few swigs.

After a moment or two Ken felt his sense of reason returning and explained to her what had taken place. He feared she might think he'd gone out of his mind, imagining things, but Eleanor was now in no doubt about the likelihood of the farmhouse being supernaturally possessed.

"I'm sorry," Ken apologised, feeling that he was letting her down by exposing a vulnerable side to his outward tough personality.

"Don't be," Eleanor sympathised, understanding that fear of the paranormal was an emotion far beyond dealing with everyday humans.

"I don't know what's gone on here in the past, but I'm sensing it was something horrific," Ken poured out his thoughts. "That woman," he paused, "that ghost gave me the deep creeps when she warned me to get out of the place." He rubbed his forehead as if that would wipe away the memory.

"I think you'd do best to leave here first thing in the morning, go home," Ken strongly advised. "I'm sure Ben will contact you as soon as he returns."

The advice coming from anyone else would not have made a compelling impression on Eleanor. But coming from Ken, unshakable in everything else she'd known him to do, needed serious consideration. If she returned home it would feel like she was abandoning her husband. However, staying at the farmhouse was a terrifying prospect.

"I can't leave the farmhouse or the area without finding Ben," Eleanor despaired, unable to make a clear choice.

"Why not see if you can stay somewhere locally," Ken suggested. "You can then still be around when Ben returns. As I'm sure he will," he added reassuringly.

"Can you handle the company's business if both Ben and me aren't there for a bit longer?" she was anxious not to load too much prolonged responsibility on him.

"Of course I can, but I'm happy to stay in some nearby accommodation too for a while to help you out here," Ken offered. "I'll even stay in this place if you want, creepy though it bloody well is." He took another swig from the beer can.

"No, I really appreciate you coming, but it's probably best if you go back and keep things running. I'll take your advice and find somewhere to stay locally for a while," she replied, forcing a smile on her troubled face.

"Whatever you want to do," said Ken. "The place has been searched, you tell me, so I don't think there's much change in either of us remaining here. No clues to find."

It came to Eleanor's mind that the outbuilding with the locked door was the only place that hadn't been searched. But the keyhole mechanism was well rusted. Ben was hardly likely to have a key, and it was unlikely he'd have locked himself inside if he did. That avenue didn't seem a prospect for offering any clue to his whereabouts.

They resolved that Ken would return home and Eleanor would find some accommodation in the village.

\*\*\*\*\*\*

KEN left in the morning only after receiving repeated assurances from Eleanor that she would not stay in the farmhouse.

After saying goodbye to him, she started packing the few items she'd brought along and putting them in the car. Then taking a last look for the time being along the track at the side, she gazed at Ben's van parked near the locked outbuilding.

Eleanor had closed the vehicle's back doors, which were wide open when she first arrived. Now, and not for the first time, she wondered why he would have gone somewhere else without closing them and locking the vehicle.

Something urgent must have happened to call him away. Surely though, he would have contacted her to say? Even if he'd decided to elope with a secret lover, it would be odd for him to leave the vehicle abandoned like that. The only other alternative was he'd been taken against his will.

Ben had upset a few rivals in the cut and thrust of business life now and then, but never to the extent they'd want to do him harm. All of them knew the name of the game. You win some, you lose some.

As the thoughts poured through Eleanor's mind, the noisy throbbing of an engine approaching the farmhouse distracted her. She walked to the front and saw a tractor arriving along the track leading up to the property. It pulled up close to her.

A young man dressed in rolled up shirt sleeves, jeans and muddy boots opened the cab door and climbed down to greet her.

"Hello, I'm Jason Coleman. I own the farm over there," he pointed to a farmhouse and cluster of barns lower down across several fields away in the distance. "I'm calling to see if I can be of any help to you."

Eleanor smiled at the neighbourly offer.

"If you could tell me where my husband is, that would be more than enough help," she replied.

"Yes, I've heard about that. News in a small place like this spreads around like wildfire," Jason sympathised with her concern. "He's a really good man. He joined our darts team the other night at the pub. Bloody good player."

It heartened Eleanor that Ben had made yet another good impression on a local, but not surprised. Ben had always been a sociable man.

"I take it the place has been thoroughly searched?" the farmer asked.

Eleanor nodded.

"I expect he'll turn up," the young man reassured her. He didn't want to delve into the possibility of partner rifts that might have led to the situation.

"Are you planning to stay here for a while, because if you want any company you're welcome to come over to my farm, have a chat with my wife, Nina. A bit of girl talk," he smiled.

The kind offer lifted Eleanor's spirits a little. What a friendly area it would be to live, if only there wasn't the present huge void in her life, and the bizarre elements attached to the farmhouse.

"Thank you. I really appreciate your offer," Eleanor returned the smile. "Right now I don't intend to spend another night in this place."

Jason could read that something strange must have occurred in the farmhouse.

"You know about its history, do you?" he asked.

"Yes, but only since I arrived here."

The bright look in the farmer's face dropped into a frown.

"I don't want to leave the area until my husband returns. I'm hoping to find some local accommodation in the village," Eleanor explained. "No way am I staying in this farmhouse on my own."

Jason's face brightened.

"I can help you there. Rose Partridge will put you up. Your husband stayed there for a while," he told her.

"Why did he stay there?"

The man's information was news to her. He paused for a moment before replying.

"Probably the same reason why you don't want to stay in the farmhouse. I take it there's been odd happenings?"

Eleanor nodded, confirming his thoughts again.

"When I get back into a phone signal area, I'll call Rose Partridge," he said decisively. "She can come across as unfriendly on the outside, but she has a heart of gold, and I'm sure she'll look after you." He gave Eleanor the woman's address.

"And if you need any help, Rose will give you my number. You're welcome to call in at my farmhouse anytime." He climbed back into the tractor cab, and starting the engine made his way back down the front track.

\*\*\*\*\*\*

Rose Partridge bared no outer thorns for Eleanor when she arrived. Jason had been in touch and filled her in about her new guest and the circumstances. Rose shared Eleanor's concern.

"He's a wonderful man," she described him, "I'm sure you miss him very much." The remark was comforting, but unintentionally emphasised Eleanor's isolation.

They sat at a table in Rose's living room with cups of tea. Animal ornaments covered the top of a dresser with more displayed on several shelves around the room. Chintz curtains drawn aside overlooked the view through the patio door on to a small paved back garden. Flowers in pots spread around the paving now drooped sadly, as their leaves and blossoms bowed to the approaching winter.

The private setting was the inner sanctum to Rose's softer side allowed only for a select few to see. Ben had shown himself to be a good, caring man, so his wife had a special pass.

"They should have demolished that farmhouse years ago. Never brought anything but trouble to people," anger showed on Rose's face. "The last owners couldn't get out fast enough. Of course, the bad spirits there waited until the Fosters' had spent a fortune on refurbishing the place before they started to appear."

The landlady's story was yet another revelation to Eleanor. If only she and Ben had known before they'd bought the place. Dry rot, damp, even structural problems. They could all have been sorted out. But hauntings? It became obvious Ben had not mentioned them because he didn't want to worry her. He was the type of person who would do everything to put things right first. Maybe that's why he was away now?

Eleanor stayed at Rose's home for a week. She was in touch with the police for updates daily, but nothing connected to his disappearance had surfaced. The best they could do was place missing person alerts on the internet and notice boards around the area.

By the end of the week, Eleanor resigned herself to the fact there was nothing more she could do by staying locally. Thanking Rose for her hospitality she returned home.

The familiar surroundings of home brought a relaxing break from the company of strangers, even though they'd all been friendly and kind. But the absence of her husband hit hard. The house seemed empty, devoid of his personality and a loving arm across her shoulders watching TV together in the evening. Little things she now realised were the shared roots of their lives.

At work, Ken insisted she she should stay away from the office for a bit longer. He could handle the day to day. Remaining idly in isolation at home, however, was not something Eleanor could tolerate.

It occurred to her that perhaps the previous owners of the farmhouse could give her more information about the place. Something they may have experienced which could give a clue to why Ben had gone missing. Probably clutching at straws, but anything that might help to find him was worth a try.

She knew Ben kept all paper documents relating to household business in a room they'd converted into a home office upstairs, and searching through a filing cabinet Eleanor found one giving the name and address of the farmhouse's previous owner. George Foster and his wife Madeleine now living in the town of Crowthorne in Berkshire. That was where they'd moved to after vacating the farmhouse and obviously left it on the market until it was sold.

The estate agent had said they were selling the farmhouse cheaply because they were planning to move abroad. But in the light of experience Eleanor knew the estate agent had not been truthful. Maybe the Fosters had moved abroad since? There was no phone number shown on the details so she couldn't check. But given that Crowthorne was only twenty five miles away, it was worth a shot.

Eleanor set off for the address early evening, deciding that people were more likely to be at home at the end of the day. Arriving an hour later, the tree lined road was visible in the darkness from the street lighting. Neat front garden hedgerows bordered most of the properties. She stopped when the satnav told her she'd reached her destination.

A gate between two hedges led down the paved footpath to the front door of the large detached house. The light from the hallway reflected off the shiny bald head of the man who answered the doorbell. Inquisitive eyes stared at her through gold rimmed spectacles. Eleanor introduced herself.

"I'm looking for George Foster. I don't know if he still lives here." Although the man was mostly in silhouette from the hall light behind, she could now see he was wearing a blue striped shirt and dark blue trousers.

"Can I ask why?"

Eleanor explained she was seeking the whereabouts of the farmhouse's previous owners. At the mention of the name Fairview Farm the man's eyes darkened as if an unpleasant memory had flashed into his mind.

"Step inside," he invited Eleanor.

The spacious hallway looked brightly welcoming with light cream walls and a large framed photograph of a ballerina.

"Who is it?" a woman in a floral dress appeared from doorway, shoulder length auburn hair and slight crease lines under her eyes. Eleanor guessed she was ten years younger than the man who looked to be in his mid sixties.

"This lady has come about that bloody farmhouse," he replied to the woman. Her face dropped.

"I'm George Foster and this is my wife Madeleine," he said, confirming Eleanor's hope of finding them. "You're going to tell me you've bought the place," the man read the reason for her visit. Eleanor nodded.

"Come into the living room."

Eleanor followed and George beckoned her to sit on the light cream armchair. Another framed photo of a nymphly, beautiful ballerina on tip-toe took pride of place above the mantelpiece, where a gas log fire burned cosily below. The television in the corner had been muted.

"That's my wife," George said proudly, seeing that the framed photo had caught Eleanor's eye.

"A long time ago," Madeleine commented wistfully.

"Tell me what's happened?" the man asked, settling on the nearby sofa with his wife.

Eleanor recounted the story of her missing husband, the creepy atmosphere and the ghostly visitation witnessed by Ken. The couple listened with intense interest, then gazed at each other knowingly for a moment.

"We had some terrible frightening times there too. The ghost of a man appearing in our bedroom in the middle of the night," said George, his face grim at the memory. "He snarled and talked to us as if we were farm workers. Then there were power cuts, flickering lights, some middle-aged woman materialising and laughing wickedly at my wife in the kitchen."

Madeleine shivered at the memory.

"And two hawks kept flying into the farmhouse whenever the front door was left open," she recalled. "They swooped at me like they wanted to peck me apart, then flew out again," the woman shook her head reliving the terror.

"Lost a lot of money on refurbishing the place," George explained. "The hauntings only started after the work had been finished. Madeleine and me hoped it would be somewhere to live in our retirement, but we had to write it off. No way would we ever go back there."

The man echoed the same plan that Eleanor had agreed with Ben as a place to spend their latter years.

"Did the estate agent tell you it had a bad history?" asked Madeleine.

"He said the previous owners were selling cheaply because they were moving abroad," Eleanor replied. The couple shook their heads at the lie Eleanor had been told.

"To be honest I was planning to have the place demolished, write it off as a loss," said George. "I've had a successful business life and could afford to take the hit just to rid the world of it." He looked thoughtful for a moment as something suddenly occurred to him.

"I did mention my idea of demolishing the farmhouse to a local in the village. It must have got passed on to the local estate agent, because a short time after he contacted me to say he was certain he could find a buyer who wouldn't mind its history if I sold at a cheap price." George shook his head again. "Stupidly I believed him."

"We're sorry if it's been landed on you," said Madeleine. "It's wrong if you weren't told about it being haunted."

Eleanor couldn't blame them. She and Ben had been duped by the agent, and right now her husband's disappearance was the greater problem in her life.

"In our experience the lounge in the farmhouse seemed to be the main area for strange events," said George. "I've thought about it on and off since and wondered if that outbuilding connected to it hides something. I never broke the lock to look inside."

The locked outbuilding had continued to nag at the back of Eleanor's mind. She didn't think Ben was trapped in there. And if he was, he could have survived in the few days before she arrived, and surely would have called for help when she'd shouted his name loudly on the track soon after. A long shot though it was, she now decided she should check, but didn't seriously think it would lead her to Ben.

Eleanor thanked the Fosters for their time and made her way back home. Shortly after returning her phone rang. It was daughter Sophie.

"Just calling to see how you and dad are," she said.

Eleanor felt put on the spot. She didn't want to say her father was missing. That would distress her. On the other hand she didn't want to lie.

"Are you alright mum?" Sophie sounded concerned by the silence that had met her.

"Yes, I'm fine," Eleanor blurted, attempting to maintain a positive front.

"You seem a bit down in the dumps."

"Just a bit tired," Eleanor maintained the air of all being normal. She was certain Ben would return and it wasn't necessary to worry her daughter.

"Dad okay?"

"Yes, he's away at the farmhouse right now. "I'll tell him you called."

"Well I hope you have better luck than me," said Sophie. "I've rung his phone several times, but I can't get a reply."

"The area's out of signal range. I'll let him know you've called as soon as he's in touch again." Eleanor wasn't lying, but she felt guilty her words carried a deception.

The women chatted for a while, mostly Sophie doing the talking.

"You do sound washed up," she told her mother after a while. "I think you're missing dad while he's away."

It was intended as a lighthearted remark, but at that Eleanor almost burst into tears. She *was* missing Ben. She fought hard to resist breaking down within earshot of her daughter. They said goodbye, then Eleanor collapsed in a bundle on the living room sofa, sobbing uncontrollably in her loneliness.

# CHAPTER 7

IN a mixture of dread and hope, Eleanor set off early next morning on the long drive to the farmhouse. Dread at the thought of returning to the place, and hope that she would discover the reason for her husband's disappearance.

She planned to get into the locked outbuilding and had taken an axe from Ben's shed at the bottom of their garden. Since there was no door key, she'd break in.

Eleanor had no intention of staying in the farmhouse. She'd rung Rose Partridge who was more than happy to accommodate her for the night, or longer if necessary.

The day had begun gloomily overcast and the temperature had continued dipping from a bitterly cold north wind. The unseasonably mild early winter weather until now was being re-balanced the other way. Flecks of snow began skirting around the car as Eleanor neared the farmhouse, grey heaps of thickening cloud casting the early afternoon light into evening.

The strengthening freeze of wind cut through her when she pulled up on the farmhouse forecourt and stepped from the car. This was not a great time for working outside as the speckles of snow began growing in size, smacking at her face.

She grabbed her overcoat and leather gloves from the passenger seat and made her way inside the farmhouse to make a warming coffee before tackling the locked outbuilding. She knew there was still a little instant coffee powder in a jar.

Through the kitchen window Eleanor could see the snow was beginning to thicken with a vengeance. She drank the coffee quickly to set about her task before it worsened.

Going to the boot of the car to collect the axe, a couple of inches of snow had already settled on the ground. Visibility was rapidly deteriorating. She'd have to work fast.

As she reached the outbuilding door, Eleanor heard the throb of a heavy engine approaching. A tractor came into view through the sweeping snow and pulled up beside her on the track.

"Eleanor?" a young man called out, climbing down from the cab. It was the farmer Jason Coleman. He saw her holding the axe.

"What's the problem?" he asked, lowering his head slightly to avoid the snow hitting his eyes.

"I want to find out what's inside this outbuilding," she replied. "How did you know I was here?"

"I saw your car across the fields going up the track while I was out herding cows towards my barn. There's terrible weather on the way. You shouldn't be out in it now."

"I've got to know what's inside this building. I have a feeling it could help me to find Ben," Eleanor insisted.

"Don't do it in this weather, you'll get stranded," Jason urged. "It could go on for days. Weather's different down here than what city folk are used to. You can stay with me and my wife Nina. As soon as it's safe I'll come back with you and help."

The snow was rapidly accumulating. Eleanor desperately wished to see what lay inside the outbuilding. She felt certain Ben wasn't there, but it could hold a key to his location.

"I'll be okay," she assured Jason, "I've arranged to spend the night at Rose Partridge's."

"Good, then I'd go there now," the farmer flinched as a strong gust smacked a flurry of snow into his eyes. "Leave it much longer and your car could get stuck in snow."

The bitter cold had begun penetrating Eleanor's coat and gloves. And now the thought of being stranded alone at the farmhouse struck terror. Even if she found a clue inside the outbuilding, she'd be unable to follow it up quickly stuck there.

"Maybe you're right," she agreed.

"Then do it now," Jason gave the order, worried for her safety. He climbed back into the tractor cab and set off.

Eleanor returned to the farmhouse feeling frustrated at the weather disrupting her plan, though she knew Jason was right. Supernatural visitations at the farmhouse chilled her more than the freezing weather.

Leaving the axe in the kitchen, she got into her car and turned the key to start the engine. It whirred, but wouldn't spark into life. Her heart sank. She tried again. The engine was at the point of bursting into life then stopped. Again and again she turned the key but the vehicle refused to start.

Now she was stuck in this bloody place from hell. No. She could walk to the village. She would not stay here. With no phone signal, there was no way to call for help.

Visibility had deteriorated even more. As Eleanor sat in the car on the forecourt, the farmhouse building, only a short distance away, was almost blotted from view in a horizontal curtain of flying snow. It seemed the farmhouse was now the only place that could offer shelter, terrifying as it was. Staying in the car she'd most likely to freeze to death.

Lowering her head against the elements, Eleanor made her way to the front door, tramping through snow that was already stacking well above her ankles. She'd never experienced such a rapid snowstorm onslaught before.

Inside, the farmhouse seemed almost welcoming compared to the penetrating cold. Snow fell from her clothing on to the hall floor. The overcast weather had virtually blocked out any daylight. Eleanor turned on the lights and heating, hoping neither unearthly spirits or power line breaks would cause them to fail.

She brought a canvas chair and the trestle table from the living room into the kitchen. Somehow it seemed the only room in the property that had less of an unwelcoming atmosphere. Then she made another warming coffee.

Her fearful uncertainty was how long she might be stranded in the place. Even if anyone realised she was still here, the weather appeared to be unrelenting. Glancing out the kitchen window, Eleanor saw visibility was down to zero. The route in and out of here would be impassable. There was no food in the farmhouse, and the snack meal she'd packed for the journey was in the car boot. Right now she wasn't venturing out to fetch it.

As she took a sip of her coffee, the lights flickered. Dread gripped her. She began to think taking a chance at finding her way to Rose's in the snow would be a better option than facing horrific hauntings in the farmhouse. Realistically she'd likely end up lost and freeze to death. But right now that seemed only marginally worse than being terrified to death.

Eleanor tried to take her mind off her imprisonment by imagining the refurbishment changes she would make to the kitchen if she and Ben had moved into the place. That is, if it was a normal home. New cabinets and overhead cupboards. The work surfaces looked too dark. She'd have to go for a lighter finish.

Laughter broke out, floating through the air. It came from one of the other ground floor rooms. Eleanor's heart started pumping furiously, her breathing growing rapid, ready to flee. But to where? Surely there was no other human being present? She listened intently. The farmhouse had fallen silent again with only the sound of the howling gale outside. Maybe the wind had sounded like laughter for a moment?

Reluctantly Eleanor left the kitchen to check the other rooms. Just to be sure no-one else was present, though she yearned for the company of another living person to drive away her loneliness. Mostly her husband Ben.

The living room was empty. She approached the lounge in terror. The room that the Foster's had said seemed to be the key location for manifestations. That too was empty, much to her relief.

As she re-entered the hallway to look upstairs, she saw two hawks perched at the top of the stairway gazing curiously at her. How on earth did they get in? Perhaps she hadn't noticed them fly inside when she'd returned to the property? They must have been desperate for shelter too.

"I haven't got any food for you," she said softly, starting to ascend the stairs towards them. She reached halfway when the birds flapped their wings, twisting round to fly in the direction of the bedroom. Eleanor scurried to the top. The bedroom door was closed. The hawks weren't present. They couldn't have flown through a closed door. Could they?

Her heart began pounding again. This is weird. She opened the door. Except for Ben's sleeping bag, the room stood empty. Eleanor looked up at the hall ceiling. Was the loft door open for the birds to have flown through? No, it was closed. Only apparitions can disappear into thin air. Surely?

The mad idea of leaving the farmhouse and finding her way to Rose's in the blizzard on foot resurfaced in her mind. It was growing into an attractive alternative to re-maining in the place. A rumble of thunder echoed outside. Panic was starting to take over. Hell seemed to be closing in on her.

Eleanor took deep breaths determined to keep control. She returned to the kitchen just as a flash of lightning brightly illuminated the snow shooting past the window. A few moments later a deafening crash of thunder vibrated through the room. The kitchen lights flickered again. Any-thing would be better than remaining here. Freezing to death now appeared better. The place was pure evil. Some-thing from hell was watching her. Toying with her. What had it done to Ben?

She needed to get a grip. Coffee wasn't strong enough. She needed an alcohol boost. Dutch courage. She looked through the cupboards and saw a beer can. As she reached for it she noticed a notebook propped between the can and the side of the cupboard.

In curiosity she took hold of it. Inside she recognised Ben's handwriting. Jotted names and phone numbers. A priest and a ghost hunter. Scribblings about an exorcism. That in itself told her a story. Ben must have had a terrible experience here. Had it driven him mad? Had he lost his mind? Was he wandering somewhere out of his head?

The frenzy in Eleanor's mind was interrupted by a sound. Was it a knock on the front door she'd heard? She listened again. Yes. Another knock came. Who could be calling in this weather? Had someone realised she was stranded? Maybe it was the farmer Jason come to check if she was okay?

Eleanor clutched at any prospect of being rescued, though surely no-one would venture out in this weather? Hope drove her to answer the call.

Snow flew at her furiously as she opened the door. For a second she saw someone standing there a few feet away, but the weather obscured a clear view. The figure appeared to turn and start moving away into obscurity. Eleanor needed to know who it was. She stepped outside, the snow almost reaching her knees. With difficulty she struggled through the deep layer following the indistinct figure.

It went round the side of the property and towards the locked outbuilding, a drift of snow now piled against the wall. Then the figure disappeared.

Eleanor reached the outbuilding door. It was now open. Something human must have opened it. Surely? What Eleanor didn't notice in the pursuit was the figure had left no footprints in the snow. She went inside.

A dim blue light partly lit the interior, just enough to see the way. Eleanor saw it shone from the gap in the false wall that Ben had breached. She stepped over a pile of rubble scattered on the ground and entered the enclosure.

Now she could see the light shining from an open door on the inside. A surge of adrenalin flushed through her. Flight or fight her senses vied for dominance. Should she proceed or get the hell out? The need to know what lay ahead drove her on.

Warily she descended the stone steps into the cellar, the light seeming to come from no visible source. A foul stench thickened the air.

Eleanor reached the bottom and looked around. She couldn't see anyone. Then she gasped in horror seeing a large pile of bones heaped against the far wall. Skulls pitched randomly among them, empty eye sockets staring.

At the front of the pile she saw a body laying on its back. There wasn't much of the body left. Mostly exposed skeletal bones and the little flesh remaining looked as though it had been viciously ripped away in pieces.

Her jaw dropped. No! It couldn't be. Eleanor saw a ring limply resting on the finger bone of the body. She stooped and took hold of the skeleton hand. It was Ben's gold wedding ring, his initials embossed on it. Eleanor noticed part of Ben's throat was still intact. Congealed blood set in a line across the remaining section. It looked like his throat had been cut. Eleanor swayed dizzily, stunned by the horror. Her mind fell into a trance trying to blot out reality. Instinct urged her to flee, sensing immediate danger.

As she turned, she caught sight of two hawks perched on a shelf recess in the wall opposite. The cold gleam in their eyes and the curved weapon of their sharp, gouging beaks emanated an aura of pure evil. Eleanor wanted to run screaming from the place, but found herself transfixed.

The hawks launched into flight, aiming directly at her. She flinched and suddenly they were gone, replaced by a grim, unshaven man in shabby clothes standing before her with a woman beside him wearing a dark grey dress, white apron and mob cap. The woman gave Eleanor a gloating smile.

"Welcome to our lair," said the man. "I am John Trevallion and this is my wife Anne."

Even in deep trauma Eleanor recalled the names the history woman, Marian Armstrong, had told her. The original owners of the farm. But they would be long dead. Eleanor's horror deepened as she realised these two were ghosts.

"We used to enjoy eating our farm workers," Trevallion delivered the revelation as if it was no more unusual than consuming an everyday meal. "They sustained us in the months of that cruel 1852 snowstorm." He looked at his wife, sharing the memory of those far off days with her. "And while the weather drove many to the brink of starvation, our workers' bodies gave us the taste for human flesh." A look of relish rose on Trevallion's face.

"Alas, since then we've no longer been able to partake of such succulent juices," the spirit looked downhearted. "But the hanging did not still us in death. Our souls remained strong, reincarnating into hawks and feeding on the meat of small field animals, mice, rats, voles, snakes."

Eleanor began to realise where the vile apparition's words were leading. She tried to move, but was unable.

"And so it was great fortune when your husband chanced upon this, our old slaughterhouse, unleashing the power of our domain," Trevallion gave a sweep with his spectral arm, bristling with pride at the gruesome sur-rounds, the bone pile and Ben's body.

"That was the chance to feast on the richness of human flesh again," Trevallion's wife Anne spoke with a grin, tast-ing the joy of what was to come. "In here we have the power to control our victims."

The thought of Ben being devoured by these vile appari-tions was more than Eleanor could bear. With the ability to change into hawks, their vicious beaks had torn his lifeless body to shreds.

"The best part was luring farm workers down here and slitting their throats," the Trevallion ghost revelled in re-calling the grisly past of his farming days. "Of course, now as birds or spirits we can't hold the deathly knife, but for that you can oblige us."

Until now Eleanor hadn't seen the sharp dagger laying on the stone slab floor a couple of feet away from Ben's emaciated body, dried blood on the blade.

Slowly she turned and moved towards the weapon. Her mind was possessed with full knowledge of what she was doing, but without the ability to stop it. She bent down and taking hold of the dagger in her right hand, she stood again to face the spectral farmer and his wife.

Her right arm rose, bringing the blade of the weapon to her throat. Her mind was forcing her to scream in terror, desperately attempting to resist the powerhold over her. But no sound came. This was to be the savage end of her life. In seconds the soft flesh of her throat would be sliced by her own hand. In the closing moment Eleanor now knew exactly what had happened to her husband.

# CHAPTER 8

JASON returned from seeing Eleanor and parked the tractor in the shelter of a barn at the rear of his farmhouse, hur-
rying through the increasing depth of snow into the warmth
of the family living room.

A cosy log fire burned in the brick fireplace as he settled
on a chair, warming his hands from the glowing heat. In an
armchair nearby his father snoozed, the old man's face
buried in a generous growth of white beard, his lips making
popping sounds between breaths.

Thick wooden beams crossed the ceiling and down the
walls. Framed family photos rested on an old mahogany
dresser. The flagstone floor was mostly covered by a red
patterned rug.

The farmhouse dated back around two hundred years
and had been home to several generations of Jason's family.
He had plans to modernise the place, but farming for him
was a hand to mouth existence. Money was not freely
available.

His wife Nina entered the room carrying two cups of tea.

"Glad you're back safely," she said, handing him a cup,
and gently tapping grandad to the couple's children on the
shoulder. He woke looking surprised for a second, wondering where he was. Then he remembered and smiling took
the cup.

Grandad's wife had died several years ago. Now he lived
alone in a small terraced house in the village.

He and his wife had moved into the rented accommodation from the farm with a view to letting their son Jason and

Nina carry on the farming business unhindered by a couple of old fogies. But now he was frequently invited to stay at the farm because the couple didn't like him being alone for too long. He was fond of Nina and thought she made the perfect match for his son.

Long, light brown hair trailed over Nina's shoulders. She was a good looking woman, though the hard life of working with her husband at the farm had slightly lined her face around the eyes and thickened her hands. She wore a long, dark red dress that was fading into retirement. Despite the meagre living, being together with their young son and daughter sustained her happiness.

After handing the men their tea, she walked across to the window.

"Never seen a snowstorm quite like this," she said, unable to see through the blanket of white to the fields beyond the window.

"We'll have to start feeding the cows in the barn. Grazing's out. Going to cost us a pretty penny," Jason replied gloomily. "The forecast is for this to last a while, and the snow depth probably won't clear for a good time after."

"Everyone round the area will be stuck inside for ages. Lucky I've got food in to last us," said Nina, turning back from the window.

"The woman whose husband is missing was back at Fairview Farm," Jason changed the subject. "I went over there and told her to leave before the weather got worse. She said she'd arranged to stay at Rose Partridge's."

"Well I hope she took your advice," Nina looked concerned. "Damned if I would stay in that God forsaken place anytime, let alone be stuck there."

"She said she'd leave shortly when I saw her. I expect she'll be alright," Jason felt certain that Eleanor taken his advice.

The room fell silent for a moment, broken soon by the old man.

"It was weather like this when it all started," he said. Both husband and wife waited for him to continue. He took a sip of his tea as if he'd concluded the thought. He often began a sentence without concluding it.

"When all what started?" Jason probed.

"The business at that place. What do they call it now? Fairview Farm." He grunted a laugh. "Dead Spirits Farm more like. That's what everyone local in the old days called it."

"What do you mean, that's when it all started?" Jason insisted. The cryptic delivery of his father was starting to annoy him.

"The cannibalism there," the old man replied.

"The what?" The couple stared at him in surprise.

"Didn't you know?" Grandad turned his gaze at them. Over the years he'd regaled his son with tales about the area and legend of local hauntings at the farmhouse. But never had he mentioned the word cannibalism. Nor had Jason or Nina heard it from anyone else.

"My father told me about it, and his father told him," the old man came into his stride of memory. "Passed down over the years, but only a few old timers in the village

112

know about it now. The young think we're making up stories."

Nina was intrigued by her elderly in-law's revelation. She drew up a chair to sit close by.

Grandad took another sip of tea, delighted by his audience gathered beside him near the warming log fire.

"It was a terrible snowstorm like this one, back in the year 1852. Went on for more than a week. Drifts ten foot high or more. No-one could move." He paused for a moment recalling his father's story. "They didn't have snow ploughs, helicopters, rescue services back then. Everyone was stranded in their farms and homes for weeks on end."

Jason was growing impatient for his father to get to the point of the story, but held back from trying to hurry him.

"John Trevallion and his wife, Anne, had some itinerant farm workers confined on that farm with them. It was a month before anyone could start venturing out again, as the snow started to melt." He took another drink of tea.

"A local girl from the village, who did daily work at the farm, made her way there to carry out cleaning, washing and general duties there. She was surprised to see the Trevallions untroubled when most other folk were downhearted, close to the point of starvation because they had practically run out of food in their homes."

Nina got up and placed another log on the fire, while grandad gathered his thoughts. He needed a moment to regain the thread. She sat again as he continued.

"The local girl noticed the three itinerant workers, who'd been there just before the snowstorm started, were no longer present on the farm. It puzzled her since they'd hardly be likely to have left for work elsewhere in the winter weather. But she thought no more of it."

A flash of lightning suddenly lit the living room window rapidly followed by a loud crack of thunder.

"The storm's overhead," said Nina looking alarmed. "I hope we don't get a lightning strike."

"Mum I'm frightened," a young fair haired girl in dark blue school uniform appeared at the living room doorway. She'd been sent home early from school along with her brother, Phillip, as the snowfall had begun to worsen. They'd settled to playing computer games upstairs in their bedrooms.

"It's okay, you're perfectly safe Heather," Nina stood up and approached her daughter, putting her arm around the girl. "The storm will pass."

Another flash and loud boom broke out as Nina comforted the girl. After a few minutes of her mother's reassurance the youngster looked more settled. She raised a smile and returned to her bedroom.

Nina went back to her chair near the fire in the hope that grandad might remember to pick up the thread of the story. He finished his cup of tea.

Jason raised his eyes to the ceiling in a look of abandonment, deciding that his elderly father's mind had wandered away into an entirely different plain.

"So the young woman helper at the farm thought no more of the itinerants not being there," Nina prompted the old man.

"That's right," he replied. His mind hadn't drifted from the tale.

"The young girl carried on at the farm for several years, and even though there was no more terrible weather like that, she noticed the itinerant labourers who'd told her they planned to stay working there awhile, suddenly seemed to disappear," the old man continued his story.

"She sometimes heard snatches of whispered conversation between the farmer Trevallion and his wife, and the horror began to dawn on her they were killing and eating the labourers. Seems they developed a taste for human flesh when they'd neared starvation in that severe winter."

Jason and Nina looked at each other, not sure if this was the rambling imagination of the elderly man, or if there was an element of truth to it.

"The girl told her mother of her suspicions, then not long after the girl disappeared too," grandad continued.

"Of course the girl's mother told the villagers what her daughter had said, and bad feeling grew about Trevallion and his wife. The two of them began to realise that rumours were mounting against them. Then one day a party of villagers raided the farm, searching for evidence of murdering. They didn't find any, but that didn't stop them hanging the couple from the branch of the old oak tree at the farm."

The old man paused for a moment, stroking his beard as if gathering his next thought.

"Some said that after they were dead and swinging at the end of the ropes, two hawks appeared on the hanging branch above them. The birds took off and flew at the villagers as if to attack, then veered away across the fields."

Nina and Jason gazed at each other again, still struggling to decide whether the story was true or just some old legend. They knew Fairview, or Dead Spirits Farm was haunted, but they'd never heard this tale about it before.

"Any chance of more tea?" grandad held out his cup.

Nina stood up and took it, deciding his story was just that. A story. Though she couldn't deny there was something unnatural about the farm. As a girl she'd ventured near the place and sensed a warning not to stay there for long.

Nina left the room to make grandad another tea when the hall landline phone began ringing. She picked up.

"Hello Rose, how are you? Coping alright with this weather?" she enquired, recognising the voice on the line. She paused for a moment. "Yes, he's in the living room. Hold on I'll get him." She called to her husband.

"Hello Rose. What's up?" Jason asked.

"I've been expecting Eleanor Telford to arrive, but she hasn't turned up yet. Getting worried she might be stuck in snow somewhere. Just wondering if you might have seen her?"

Jason explained that he'd called in at the farmhouse not long ago. That Eleanor said she was leaving shortly to make her way over.

"Oh dear, I hope she's safe. This isn't the time to be stranded somewhere," the woman's concern was palpable.

"Christ, I hope she isn't stuck at the farmhouse. It's impossible to travel at the minute. Even the authorities are probably locked down," Jason shared Rose's concern. "Let me know if she turns up," he said, worried it was becoming a remote possibility.

Nina was listening and gathered the gist of the conversation. The concern was spreading to her. Jason ended the call.

"She should have bloody well taken my advice and left the place straightaway. I blame myself. I should have just lifted her up and put her in the tractor."

"Don't be ridiculous, it's not you fault," Nina attempted to soothe him. Jason paced around the hall in turmoil.

"There's nothing else for it. I'll have to get the tractor out and go there. This weather's going on for ages. The poor woman could starve or freeze to death," he made his decision.

"Now you are being bloody ridiculous," Nina grew angry. "Even in the tractor you won't get far. You'll end up stuck and freezing to death."

"I can't just sit by knowing the woman could be dead when all this clears. How would you expect me to live with myself?"

Nina was inwardly tearing apart. She knew Eleanor couldn't just be abandoned. But she didn't want to lose the love of her life. Her children to be left without a father.

"My tea ready yet?" grandad's voice boomed from the living room. Nina was seized with a desire to smash the cup she held over the old man's head. She resisted. The terror of her husband never returning overrode all. He planned a mission of madness.

"I will be back, my love," Jason took her in his arms. "Make sure the kettle's on so I can join you and grandad for a cup of your wonderful tea."

Nina joined him in the side lobby by the front door where Jason put on his overall and boots.

"You know I have to do this," he kissed her and opened the front door. For a moment it was forced back by a howling gust of flying snowspray. Heaving it shut behind him, he stooped against the furious onslaught as a flash of lightning and crashing thunder greeted him.

Jason trudged across to the barn with snow piling against the doors. He struggled to open them against the deepening layer, but managed enough space to drive out the tractor. The cab offered protection from the weather, though the sweep of the wipers barely showed the way ahead for more than a few seconds, which was limited anyway.

Only Jason's local knowledge of the protruding snow covered shapes around him, fences, trees and hedgerows made it possible for him to progress slowly. The vehicle's headlights were useless for guidance. But illumination thrown up by the snow layers turned out to be useful, with frequent flashes of lightning aiding visibility.

A normal ten minute journey by tractor to reach the track leading up to the farmhouse turned into half-an-hour. Even the deep traction on the vehicle's tyres were struggling not to give way to sliding.

Another quarter mile up the track incline to the farm took another quarter hour. Jason sank nearly up to his knees as he climbed out the tractor cab on to the buried forecourt. Through the thick curtain of snow he could just about see a light in the building's front window.

A large mound of snow covered what appeared to be the shape of a car parked nearby. Eleanor must have got stranded here, but at least from the light Jason guessed she was safe inside the farmhouse.

Now a normal stroll across the forecourt became a physical effort to move, each step a haul in and out of the white depth. Jason reached the front door. It was wide open with blown snow piled into the hallway. That was his first indication something was wrong.

"Eleanor?" he called, stepping inside. "Mrs Telford?"

No reply.

Jason began searching the rooms continuing to call out to her. He went upstairs. The bedrooms were empty save for the sleeping bags and some clothes piled on the floor. Where was she?

The lights flickered. Jason knew it was highly likely the storm could bring down many power lines. The place could soon be plunged into darkness.

Maybe Eleanor had left the farmhouse some way other than using her car. But that didn't seem feasible. He'd come all this way to discover she wasn't here. He could hardly do a thorough search of the farmhouse surrounds in this weather. But something was not right.

With a heavy heart, feeling he'd somehow failed the woman by not delivering her into safety, there was nothing else left for now but to begin the hazardous journey home. Another flash of lightning and instant crash of thunder shaking the farmhouse indicated the storm was right overhead, the bolt possibly striking somewhere nearby.

Jason stood at the front door preparing to leave and head towards the tractor. As he stepped into the snow, he noticed small dips in the layer leading off to the side of the property. They appeared to have been made by earlier footmarks now almost covered by the snow.

Were they Eleanor's? Had she seen or heard something that made her leave the farmhouse so urgently that she'd left open the front door? Surely there would be a trace of other footprints if anyone else had been there too?

Jason braced himself against the weather and decided to follow the trail. It led him round the side to the stone outbuilding, now with a high drift of snow piled almost to the roof. The imprints along here had been entirely buried, but he noticed the storeroom door was wide open, the snow piling up inside from the driving blizzard.

He entered the building and saw a dim blue light coming from a gap in the side wall. He approached and nearly tripped on the pile of rubble below it.

Jason began to feel tension mounting. The strange legend of Fairview, or Dead Spirits Farm, rose into his thoughts. He was a rational man, but this was weird. A light coming from a gap in the inside wall of an old outbuilding in the middle of a ferocious storm. For a moment instinct told him to flee. But what if Eleanor was here? He needed to know what lay beyond.

Stepping inside the enclosure he approached the source of the glowing light from the open door to the side, every nerve in his body tensing as he descended the stone steps leading into the unknown.

Halfway down he saw Eleanor gripping a knife, the blade poised ready to sweep a deadly slash across her throat. Two figures stood before her witnessing the spectacle.

"No!" he leapt down the steps rushing at her and grabbing her arm to pull the knife away. The action shook Eleanor out of her trance. She stared at the knife in her hand with horror, then threw it aside.

"We have another one to satisfy our pleasure," the voice of spirit Trevallion boomed, drawing Jason's attention to his presence and the woman beside.

Jason immediately assumed these strangers had somehow forced Eleanor into an act of suicide. Drugged her perhaps. The logic of supernatural influence didn't dawn on him in the split second calculations racing through his mind. He leapt to attack the man, determined to floor him, but found himself flying through the spirit and crashing to the ground. Then dread struck him. The man and woman were the ghosts of Dead Spirits Farm.

The couple laughed as Jason got up. The farmer stared at them in terror. He had no defence against entities from the world beyond. Eleanor was approaching to be beside him, but stopped in her tracks as Jason began to feel something taking possession of his body, controlling his movement. Consciousness of the surroundings starting to slip away.

He was vaguely aware of retrieving the dagger from the ground, but even that sensation was fading. As he and Eleanor drifted into a trance of helplessness, an almighty blast of thunder shook the air, reaching into the depths of the grisly cellar.

Outside the blinding flash of lightning lit the snow covered farmstead like a thousand suns.

The strike hit the old tree at the bottom of the side track, savagely splitting it apart. As the halves broke away, the lower branch reputed to have swung the Trevallions by the neck smashed into the snow depths, violently snapping from the trunk with a resounding crack.

The haze that had clouded Jason and Eleanor's minds started to clear. Jason became aware he was holding the dagger close to his throat. In horror he flung it away.

John Trevallion and his wife seemed confused, troubled, looking around uncertainly, the gloating triumph in their faces wiped away.

Eleanor was the first to notice a shimmering white mist rising from her husband's decimated body. It swirled and began to take shape, forming into the perfect image of Ben. He smile at her.

Shimmering white mist began rising from the piles of bones stacked behind him. Jason gazed at the spectacle, unsure if this was reality or a vivid nightmare. Shapes of men in ragged clothes, unshaven faces, vengeful eyes started to materialise.

Eleanor reached out to embrace Ben, but her arms went through him clutching at air. Ben's attention was focused on the Trevallions, who were now backing away in fear. He advanced towards them, the risen souls of the long departed itinerant labourers spreading out on each side of him to surround their murderers.

In a circle the spirits closed in on the terrified couple, arms reaching out to deal violent justice like a crowd baying to tear the hated victims apart.

Trevallion and his wife sank to the ground under the onslaught, as the spirits all began dissolving into white mist, evaporating through the floor. Jason and Eleanor stared at the spot, stunned.

Eleanor could never know the prophetic words that the priest, Father O'Connor had said to Ben about the evil. *'Only deep love can lead the tormented spirits to rise against the horror.'*

Neither would she know the deep love that existed between her and Ben powerfully transcended the grave, sparking retribution against the evil spirits and saving both herself and Jason's life.

Gradually their senses were restored, but the event still seemed bizarrely unreal. The stark display of ghosts from beyond.

Eleanor started to feel dizzy. She tottered. Jason took hold of her and carried her up the stairs. The snow was not as intense, but visibility remained limited.

He wondered if they should take shelter in the farmhouse, although that would leave them cut off from the outside world for some time. And Eleanor needed proper care. She had fallen unconscious and looked pale. He feared for her life. No, he'd have to chance getting her back to his farm on the tractor. There was no certain choice. Staying or leaving were fraught with perils.

As he carried her in his arms, the escape faced new difficulty. The snow depth now reached Jason's knees and awkward high strides, coupled with the ferocious wind driving freezing flakes into his eyes, forced him to use every resource his muscles could render in battling towards the tractor.

The cab was designed for one occupant and Jason had no choice but to fit her, knees drawn up to her chest, in a small space behind the seat. The snow had piled considerably higher round the wheels since he'd left the vehicle and Jason feared even their large size and deep tread would be unable to shift.

Edging the tractor forward, he could hear the engine struggle and the tyres beginning to slip. He eased off then nudged into reverse a little. Repeating back and forward movements he made a trench in the track. Now using the length of the trench, he revved at speed, breaking through the barrier of heaped snow.

His heart skipped a beat as several times the wheels started sliding. The key was to maintain momentum. Many of the hedgerow landmarks had now disappeared under drifts and only the snow laden height of trees on route stood out. Thankfully he knew the layout of these marker points across the landscape from boyhood.

Totally exhausted he eventually drew the tractor to a halt as close to the front door of his farmhouse as possible. He lifted Eleanor out of the cab just as his wife Nina opened the door. She was overwhelmed with relief that her husband hadn't perished in the storm.

Inside the farmhouse, Jason placed Eleanor on the living room sofa. Nina's expression of joy seeing her husband safely home had changed to worry.

"What's happened?" she asked, seeing Eleanor laying there unconscious.

"I'll tell you in a while, just make up a bed in the spare room she needs rest."

Nina left the room and hurried upstairs. Jason heard his wife calling to the children as she made her way to the spare bedroom.

"Dad's back. He's safe. But stay in your rooms for the minute while we sort some things out."

Eleanor's complexion had turned deathly white. For a moment Jason thought she might be dead. He took hold of her wrist to check her pulse. It faintly throbbed. He breathed a sigh of relief. She needed medical help, but the prospect of anyone being able to get there was not good. However, he had to try.

He took the phone from his inside coat pocket. No signal. He tried the landline in the hall. The line was dead. They were cut off from the outside world.

Back in the living room he noticed his wife had taken the precaution of putting a torch on the dresser, a pile of candles and two LED lanterns that Jason sometimes used to check round the barns on winter nights. The room lights still worked, but a power cut could happen any time.

Nina returned and Jason carried Eleanor up to the spare bedroom. It was a small room, rarely used, and apart from the bed and a cabinet beside, it had no other furnishings.

Jason's father appeared at the door behind them as Nina tucked Eleanor comfortably in bed. He'd been in the kitchen with the door closed, listening to the radio and eating a sandwich Nina had made for him.

"What's happened?" he asked.

"I'll tell you in a while," Jason waved off further enquiry.

"You look flat out," the old man observed.

"I am bloody flat out. I just need some rest," Jason replied sharply. He left and made for his bedroom, stripping off his soaking clothes and slumping on to the bed and collapsing into a deep sleep.

Nina spoke to the children assuring them all was well, then went downstairs to join the youngster's grandad by the fireside.

As they sat wondering what on earth could have happened, the lights went out. Nina lit a few candles placing them around the room, then using the torch took two lanterns upstairs for the children's bedrooms.

When she returned downstairs, grandad had fallen asleep in the armchair. Not wishing to disturb him, she joined her exhausted husband in bed, but got up frequently through the night to check on Eleanor's condition. A little colour was restoring to her cheeks. At least that was a good sign.

Nina hardly slept, wondering what had happened. She knew her husband would be exhausted battling through the blizzard. But Eleanor's condition? Perhaps he'd found her wandering lost in the snowstorm and overcome with cold. She had to wait until the following morning to find out, the day dawning overcast, but snow no longer falling. Now just a bitter wind whipping up swirls from the deep covering.

Jason was a strong man, though the ordeal had left him drained of his usual energy. He settled by the living room fire with his wife and grandad to recount the harrowing experience at the farmhouse. While to many audiences his story would been credited as the tale of a madman, his family didn't doubt his word. Nor would most of the village folk when the story got out.

"The heap of bones must be the itinerants that Trevallion and his wife cut up to eat. I told you my father and his father's story was right," the old man took satisfaction in what he considered confirmation of the family tale.

"Poor Eleanor. What a way to find her husband. No wonder she's in deep shock," Nina shook her head in heartfelt sympathy. "And you..." Nina looked at her husband, her words trailing away at the thought of Jason almost perishing at that cursed farm. She sat beside him on a chair. He took her hand and smiled at her. For a few moments they remained silent in thought.

"But why was part of that outbuilding bricked up?" Jason wondered, returning to the event.

"I imagine when the local girl who helped out there started talking about her suspicions, the Trevallions got word the locals were ganging up against them," grandad suggested. "They probably wanted to make sure no-one would find any evidence. Didn't stop them getting hanged though."

Several days passed before the family could communicate again with anyone outside, as snow ploughs began to clear roads to the surrounding farms, and phone connections were restored.

Eleanor gradually grew stronger and was able to join the family after spending days of complete rest, although the loss of her husband and dreadful memory of seeing his decimated body continued to deeply affect her. Everyone did their best to try and prevent her descending into a state of morose depression. But the healing would be a slow process, and Nina insisted she stay with them for the time being.

Now Eleanor began to feel the pressing need to tell her son and daughter of their father's passing. How could she say he'd cut his throat at the behest of ghosts and his body torn apart? They'd think she was mad.

She rang and felt terrible telling them the lie their father had been depressed for some time with business worries and had taken his own life while working on the farm renovations.

"I'll come straightaway," her daughter Sophie said.

"Right, I'll book a flight and come over," son Michael in Australia reacted.

"No, not yet," Eleanor put them off. "They have to carry out an autopsy. It'll be a while before his body is released for us." Now she felt even worse. "I'll let you know when to come."

Both son and daughter thought their mother's instructions a bit odd, but agreed to her wish. One day she'd have to tell them what really happened, and they'd think her deranged. But that would have to wait.

# CHAPTER 9

ELEANOR was right about the authorities wanting to carry out an autopsy on Ben's body and uncover the mysterious circumstances of his death. A week later a police Land Rover ploughed through the diminishing snow layer leading up to the farm and stopped out front.

Jason had reported the grim find at Eleanor's farmhouse and was coming out of a barn as the vehicle pulled up. He invited the two uniformed officers, a stern looking woman in her late forties and a younger male officer, into the living room.

Nina offered them coffee, but they declined, serious investigative expressions fixed on their faces.

Jason recounted what had happened, but didn't mention any supernatural influences, just that he'd gone to find Eleanor and discovered her in the cellar suffering deep shock at finding her husband's body. She'd seen the outbuilding door open and went inside from curiosity. They'd never believe a paranormal tale.

The officer's looked doubtful and asked to see Eleanor, who was upstairs resting. Nina left to fetch her. Eleanor entered the room a few minutes later looking drawn, the horrifying memory still haunting her.

The police officers could see she was burdened with distress, but expressed no sympathy to her for the loss. They concentrated on enquiry. How she and Jason had come across Ben's body and the heap of bones in the cellar? What was the relationship between Jason and her? Had Eleanor argued with her husband before he took his own life?

Eleanor wanted to tell them about the supernatural events, but knew it would be dismissed as rubbish. She was starting to wonder if the officers suspected she and Jason had murdered Ben in some jealous lovers' tryst. They were years apart in age. Surely the police couldn't think that?

The officers asked who had discovered the false wall in the outbuilding and broken through it. Eleanor assumed it was Ben. She'd noticed the sledgehammer he owned laying on the ground when she entered the building.

After more questioning the officers looked at each other seeming not to be convinced with what they'd heard. The policewoman addressed them in serious tone.

"I would like you both to accompany us to the police station," the polite delivery belied the order.

Nina had remained silent until that moment, quietly annoyed at the officers' total lack of concern for what Eleanor had endured.

"This woman has just lost her husband," Nina approached Eleanor placing a protective arm round her shoulders. "My husband has risked his life to save her. Why are you treating them like criminals?" her anger poured out.

Grandfather, who'd been in his room upstairs, came down to witness the scene.

"What's going on?" He saw the officers and sensed something was wrong from the tense faces and atmosphere.

"They want to take Eleanor and Jason to the police station," Nina told him

"Why? They've done nothing wrong," he looked bewildered.

The officers were becoming agitated at the opposition building against them.

"Don't make any trouble. We are conducting routine enquiries," said the policewoman, raising her hand to quell the mounting rebellion.

The family knew they couldn't stop the processes of the law without creating a worse situation, and reluctantly conceded. As they left, the children, Heather and Phillip, who'd been upstairs, asked why daddy was being taken away by the police. They were troubled.

"It's alright," their mother reassured them," he'll be back soon." Nina sincerely hoped that was true.

At the police station in a town ten miles away, a grim looking, grey-haired detective sergeant interviewed them seperately in turn. From the questioning it became more apparent to both that they were suspected of having an affair. That Ben had been a stumbling block to them living together and that they'd conspired to murder him.

"I'm nearly forty years older than Jason, why in God's name do you think he would want to settle for a life with me when he has a loving wife and children?" Eleanor exploded in fury when she realised the angle the detective was pursuing. "I loved my husband, and still do, with all my heart," she broke down in tears.

Jason's disbelief in the direction of his interview also made him boil with anger.

"I suppose as well as having an affair with Eleanor, I killed her husband and planned to dump his body on the bone pile of people I've been murdering on and off for nearly two hundred years." Jason shook his head at the ludicrous line the detective was pursuing.

Both of them were left alone in their separate interview rooms for nearly an hour. Then an officer told them they were free to go, but not to leave the vicinity of Jason's farmhouse while enquiries continued.

"Well you brought us here, so you can take us back," Jason ordered, still fuming at the mistreatment he and Eleanor had received. After ten minutes they were led to a Land Rover and driven back to the farm.

Eleanor remained at the farmhouse for a few more weeks, gradually regaining her strength. When news came that no charges would be made against her or Jason, the family sighed with relief. Forensics determined Ben had taken his own life and his body largely decimated by vermin. Tear marks made by birds puzzled them, but it was assumed they'd found access through some unseen opening. The bone pile was confirmed as the remains of people who'd died in suspicious circumstances a long time ago.

Now being free to leave the area, Eleanor was beginning to feel like an interloper in the family's everyday lives. She announced her decision to return home. The early snap of unusually ferocious winter cold was receding and normal movement was rapidly resuming.

Jason took her back to the hateful farmhouse to see if he could get her car started. They were filled with foreboding at the prospect of revisiting the horrific memory, but strangely the dark atmosphere seemed to no longer hover over the setting.

It didn't take Jason long to fix a loose wire in the car's electrics and start the engine. Eleanor hadn't intended going into the farmhouse to collect possessions, but a sixth sense told her there was no longer anything to fear about the place. Against her earlier instincts to leave immediately, she decided to take a last look inside the property.

"Are you sure?" asked Jason, concerned the move would cause her to break down. She nodded. They entered.

In the living room dirt marks covered the carpet where police boots sodden with snow had tramped around. The trestle table and chairs had been removed. The kitchen had been thoroughly searched, cupboards doors and drawers left open with some crockery laying smashed on the floor.

They went into the most threatening room. The lounge. Daylight streaming down the hall from the open front door provided light denied by the boarded window. Eleanor would never know the evil force of the Trevallions that had smashed the window to pieces.

However, now there was no unnatural atmosphere about the room. A gloomy veil seemed to have lifted. But the short visit was enough. Eleanor didn't want to chance the possibility of another horrific visitation.

As Jason led her out, she stopped for a moment, something catching her eye through the open door of the living room. A figure. It was Ben! He smiled at her. Eleanor's jaw dropped. She made to approach him. The figure was gone.

"What's the matter?" Jason turned back, realising Eleanor wasn't following him.

"I've just seen him," her face widened in awe.

"Who?"

"My husband. Ben."

Jason stepped back to look in the empty room, wondering if the shock from everything that had happened was prompting Eleanor's mind into wishful thinking. But then he'd seen ghosts. Maybe she had seen her husband's spirit. Maybe not.

"I just want to look round the side," said Eleanor, now starting to feel unafraid of entering the track that had led to the horror.

"Are you sure?" Jason grew concerned that Eleanor might be losing it. She ignored his caution and began making her way. Jason followed.

She approached the outbuilding and saw the door had been fitted with a hasp, secured by a sturdy padlock. It didn't matter. Eleanor didn't feel strong enough to revisit the interior. Jason stood nearby, not worried only for Eleanor's state of mind. He was finding proximity to the building raising his own stress level.

"Look!" Eleanor cried. She pointed to the field at the end of the track. "The tree. It's down."

Jason gazed in surprise. He followed as she made her way towards it.

The split main trunk bowed outwards, the branches on each side almost touching the thawing snow on the field. The broken hanging branch no longer vaunted its dark past, now laying flattened on the ground. Scorch lines delivered by the lightning strike ran down the insides of the divided trunk and the bark on the felled branch had been turned to charcoal by the mighty electrical charge.

Eleanor and Jason stared at the ruins for a moment or two, both sensing that somehow an evil had been struck down too. No rational explanation for the feeling, just a deep sensation in their souls. Eleanor turned to her companion.

"Will you finish the job started by nature and burn that branch and tree for me? They are beyond redemption now, in more ways than one."

Jason promised he would.

Eleanor stayed for lunch with the family then bid them farewell, making her return journey back home. As she travelled, a growing sense of loneliness descended. She began to miss the company of the kindest people she'd ever known. The miles also seemed to be taking her further away from Ben. She could swear she'd seen him smile at her in the farmhouse.

Ken Wainwright, the office manager, came to visit her daily at home and make sure she was coping. She explained to him what had happened and he didn't doubt it, having experienced a haunting there himself. And he understood that few others would believe her. Though he wished she'd left the place when he'd cautioned her, and not suffered the horror.

After a couple of weeks Eleanor returned to work where everyone expressed their sorrow for her loss. She immersed herself in the business again, but her heart was no longer in it. At night she returned to the emptiness of home, realising how even mundane everyday moments she'd spent with Ben were among the most precious times of their life together.

The truly hard part was when her son and daughter and the wider family arrived for Ben's funeral. His body, or what remained of it, had been released after all enquiries had been completed and brought back home for the service at the local church.

She felt terrible about continuing the lie that he'd committed suicide, weighed down by business worries.

"Why would dad want to take his own life in that horrible place?" daughter Sophie questioned her mother after the funeral. By now the story of the grisly find of bones and Ben's death in the farmhouse cellar had surfaced in the media.

"I don't know," Eleanor could only reply. She couldn't tell her daughter that evil supernatural forces had made him cut his throat. Sophie and the family would never believe it. They'd think his death had driven her insane.

It was a great relief to Eleanor when everyone finally left to return home. The pressure of suppressing the truth was becoming unbearable.

A few more weeks passed and the feeling that had been growing ever more strongly in her rose to the surface. Ben was still at the farmhouse. She was convinced. He was calling to her. In dreams, he beckoned. They could still spend happy days in retirement together.

Next day in the office she spoke to Ken.

"Would you like to take over the business?" she asked.

Ken looked stunned. He'd never considered such a proposition, though he was experienced enough to take charge.

"Why? What are you planning?"

"I'm planning to return where I know happiness lies," Eleanor replied enigmatically.

Ken shook his head in amazement.

"I know you think I'm mad, but I know Ben's there," her eyes sparkled. "The evil has gone."

The man did think Eleanor's loss had affected her mind, but she seemed happy. What if she was mad? A happy state of madness was far better than the depths of despair.

Ken didn't have the money to buy the business outright, but Eleanor was content to sign it over on the basis of the company paying her a percentage of profits.

She put her house in High Wycombe on the market and made plans to move back to Fairview Farm.

Rose Partridge welcomed Eleanor on her return to the village, and she stayed at Rose's house while making arrangements to have the farmhouse furnished. She also instigated works for the dreaded cellar to be filled in with concrete and the outbuilding demolished, removing all physical trace of the horrifying past.

Jason and his family were thrilled to see Eleanor join their community. She was now truly one of them.

When she finally moved into the farmhouse, Ben was there to greet her. Of course, no-one else could see or hear him, but that was a private affair between the re-united couple.

# OTHER BOOKS BY THE AUTHOR

I hope you enjoyed *Dead Spirits Farm.* If you would like to read more of my books they are listed below and available through Amazon. But first a taste of my popular novel:

# DEADLY ISLAND RETREAT

THERE are times in life when you wish you could turn back the clock. Reset the moment when you agreed to do something that seemed a good idea at the time, only later to find it was a big mistake.

That's how the episode began after an old friend, Lawrence Keating, rang me one day.

"Alex, how are you keeping? I've bought an island off the west coast of Scotland. Come and spend a few days with me."

Lawrence was the only person I knew who would have enough money to buy an island. We'd met five years earlier at a business college. The fact that we were both aged 22 and shared the same birth date in May had instantly connected us.

He was the flyaway student, brilliant in sales and marketing strategies to the extent his knowledge often exceeded the tutors. But he was modest with it. Friendly, the life and soul of the party. No-one could be envious or annoyed with him.

"You've bought an island? That's amazing." I was impressed, though not surprised Lawrence could do something like that.

"It's not exactly a sun-baked paradise island, but fantastically atmospheric," he said. "There's an old mansion there that needs a lot of renovation, but I've got plans in hand for it. Come and meet me."

As it happened I was between jobs. That is, having recently lost my job as manager of an office equipment store which had gone into liquidation. I wasn't a brilliant student like Lawrence, but the difference in ability didn't stop us from enjoying each other's company at the college.

"Where should I meet you and when?" I asked.

"Why now. No time like the present. I've got a motor launch moored at an old fishing harbour at Tullochrie on the north west coast of Scotland. The island's about five miles offshore there. It's called Fennamore. You might have heard of it."

I hadn't, but then I wasn't an expert on Scottish islands.

"It's a long drive from London. It'll have to be tomorrow," I told him. "I've a few things to sort out."

"All right. Tomorrow. There's a pub by the harbour called the The Ship Inn. I'll meet you there."

"It'll be about two o'clock," I said.

"Okay, but don't be late. See you then." Lawrence hung up.

That was him all over. Driving people to agree to something before they'd hardly had a chance to take it in. That was the secret of his success.

Fortunately his invite had come at the right time. Being between jobs I had a bit of time to spare. There were a couple of interviews lined up, but not for another week. And I hadn't seen Lawrence in over a year. It would be good to meet up again.

My girlfriend, Rosie, was away on a training course from work and wouldn't be back for a few days. She was in sales for a cosmetics company and forging ahead with a great career. By coincidence, her course was only sixty miles away from the coastal town in Scotland where I'd agreed to meet Lawrence.

It was an eight-hour-drive from my London flat in Fulham and I arrived at Tullochrie just before two o'clock. Lawrence was standing outside The Ship Inn, wearing black chinos and a light blue shirt patterned with yachts and motor boats. The seafaring theme had obviously grabbed him.

His fair hair, blue eyes and square jawline gave him an assertive look that immediately instilled confidence. You could see how this would literally give him a head start in convincing business partners and customers that he was their man.

"Alex, you wonderful person. It's fantastic to see you again," he greeted me with a hug. "Isn't this an amazing place."

I looked around, taking in the colourful boats bobbing gently on the harbour water, seagulls gliding in the breeze, and the rippling sea beyond stretching to the horizon. Grey stone cottages bordered the harbour front and sides, with narrow lanes at each end leading into the small town behind.

"Inspirational isn't it?" Lawrence placed his arm around my shoulders. "So great to see you again."

He was always over the top with everything. But that was his magnetic charm.

"Making loads of money?" he asked.

"Not exactly at this minute," I answered honestly.

"Never mind," he smiled. "I can give you a steer to some amazing investments. Make you rich overnight."

"Great," I replied. "But right now I feel really knackered after a long drive. Can we get something to eat?"

"Sorry, sorry. I'll buy you lunch. Come on."

We entered the pub and after boosting my system with steak pie and chips downed with a beer I felt renewed.

As we made our way along the harbour to where Lawrence's 30-foot, blue and white motor launch Pioneer was berthed, he recited all the technical details about the boat. He'd already filled my head with many of its features over lunch. His enthusiasm was unstoppable.

If only I'd know what was to come, I'd have turned back at that moment and driven home to London. As it was, my horrific future was already unfolding.

Outside the harbour the sea was choppy and the launch bounced furiously over the waves. I wasn't the best seafarer and my stomach began to protest.

Lawrence was in his element.

"Yippee," he yelled, and accelerated causing the craft to whack into the waves even harder.

"Soon be there," he called to me from the wheel, as I sat on the deck enduring the violent impact and feeling like death.

"There's Fennamore island!" he shouted excitedly a short while later. I glanced ahead. The outline of the island was partly covered in a blue-grey mist, giving it a mysterious, almost threatening appearance, as if a warning to stay away.

"I own that," Lawrence announced loudly, bristling with pride as he began turning the launch towards a small inlet. The opening led to a curved pebbly bay with a projecting stone jetty to the side. The bay waters were calmer and with the boat no longer furiously bouncing I began to feel better. Lawrence steered the craft alongside the jetty.

"There's the house," he pointed to a large greystone mansion, which it would be difficult to miss given its size. The steeply pitched slate roof was pitted with extensive patches of moss. A ledge spanned the building just below the roof line with gargoyles perched on each side of the facing corners, fanged teeth and vicious claws projecting into the skyline.

The building loomed at the top of a steep slope overlooking the bay. I felt uncomfortable in its towering presence. The tall, leaded-light front windows seemed to peer curiously like a collection of eyes assessing the new arrival to their island domain.

Lawrence had no such qualms.

"Come on, let's get inside," he called tying the boat ropes to capstans on the jetty. I grabbed my overnight bag and followed.

We walked up the steep gravel track dividing a wide grass slope rising to the house. The view on each side as we neared the top opened across fields and a distant spread of pine trees to the right shrouded in mist.

Crunching yet more gravel underfoot across the broad forecourt at the top, we reached a short flight of steps taking us to the stately oak door entrance.

"Isn't it amazing," Lawrence continued to enthuse.

"Yes," I agreed, "but you've definitely got your work cut out."

As we grew closer to the building I could see much of the stonework was eroding with age and neglect, cracks in places and the wood frames on many of the windows rotting.

"I've got great plans for this place," Lawrence's spirit was undeterred. "Just needs money and a lot of TLC. The last owner Lord Ernest Loftbury died broke. The place had been falling apart for years. That's how I got the island and house for a knock down price. No-one could see its potential like me."

The oak front door began to open. An elderly man in a white, open neck shirt and grey trousers appeared. There was no sign of welcome on his grizzled face, merely an unemotional stare.

"This is Andrew McKellan, my butler, caretaker and general maintenance man," Lawrence introduced him. "And this is our guest, Alex Preston, a good friend of mine from college days," he announced, slapping me on the shoulder.

The man just nodded acknowledgement of my presence and held out his hand to take my travel bag.

"Andrew will drop that in your room and his wife, Laura, will bring us some coffee and cakes in the sitting room." Lawrence beckoned me inside as his employee disappeared inside with my bag.

The entrance hall was huge. A vast candelabra hung above the setting, attached to a chain stretching two-storeys up to the roof. Dark wood panelling filled the expanse, with a wide stairway to the right sweeping up to balconies overlooking the hall on the first and second floors.

It was a grand setting, but now tarnished with age. Many of the glass beads in the candelabra were missing and the remainder coated in dust. The panelling and several doors off the hallway looked faded and scuffed.

Within moments of us entering an elderly, grey-haired woman emerged from a side passage at the back of the hall. She was wearing a green apron scattered with patches of flour and held a ladle in her left hand.

"This is Laura, Andrew's wife," my host made the next introduction to me. The woman wasn't as impassive in her greeting as her spouse, raising the semblance of a smile in her craggy, aged face, but was far from overwhelmed by my arrival.

"Laura is an amazing cook," Lawrence placed his arm around her shoulders, which made the woman look distinctly uncomfortable. I gained the impression husband and wife bore some sort of resentment towards us.

She ducked from under Lawrence's embrace and returned down the passageway.

"Where did you find them?" I whispered to him. They didn't look like people he would choose to suit his outgoing personality.

"They're old family retainers. I'll tell you about it later," he whispered back, then walked across to one of the doors off the hall.

"Come in here," he opened it. "This is the former sitting room."

More dark panelling surrounded the large room with a bay window at the far end. It was empty apart from a brown leather sofa and a couple of armchairs.

The broad fireplace was ornately fashioned with a carved wood mantelpiece surround. Above it hung the portrait of a middle-aged man with a bushy, dark moustache and neat side parted hair. He stared down at us austerely, an air of superiority in his gaze. Lawrence saw me studying the oil painting.

"That's the late Lord Ernest Loftbury. A gentleman of the English aristocracy and the last in a long bloodline to own the island."

An uneasy feeling that the lord in the portrait was somehow not gone from the place came over me. His image seemed so alive. Penetrating, calculating eyes.

"This will make a great conference room," Lawrence surveyed the setting, his enthusiasm unbounded.

"Conference room?" I was puzzled.

"Yes, I plan to turn the place into a getaway for businesses. Where executives can find relaxation as well as getting down to the nitty gritty of sales expansion strategies. An island retreat."

"It's not exactly a sunny isle," I pointed out.

"That's the point." Lawrence walked across to the bay window overlooking the side of the property. "It's for mental and physical toning. There's another large ground floor room that I'll convert into a gym and sauna. And another for a swimming pool. This place is enormous. Twenty upstairs bedrooms alone."

His imagination was soaring. I had to admire his get up and go.

"And, of course, loads of room on the island for a boot camp, outward bound, golfing, tennis and sailing from the bay. The potential's enormous." He paused. "But there's a lot to clear up and renovate first."

I joined him at the bay window. The large lawn outside and flower beds were overgrown with weeds.

"But it can all be done."

At that moment Laura entered the room with a tray of coffee and cakes, placing it on a small table in front of the sofa.

"Let's have a quick bite and drink, then I'll take you for a tour round the island in the launch before it gets dark."

As we settled down on the sofa for the snack, I felt distinctly uncomfortable with Lord Loftbury staring at us from the portrait.

*Alex's discomfort turns to horror, when the grisly secrets of the island begin to emerge. Discover the horrifying events in DEADLY ISLAND RETREAT. Available on Amazon.*

THE ANARCHY SCROLL

A race against time to save the world in a dangerous lost land.

**All books available on Amazon**

For more information or if you have any questions
please email me:
**geoffsleight@gmail.com**

Or visit my Amazon Author page:
**amazon.com/author/geoffreysleight**

Tweet me at: **http://twitter.com/resteasily**

Your views and comments are welcome and appreciated.

Printed in Great Britain
by Amazon